Lord Fournier's Shameless Princess

Scarlett Affairs
Book 4

Cerise DeLand

ARE YOU SIGNED UP FOR DRAGONBLADE'S BLOG?

You'll get the latest news and information on exclusive giveaways, exclusive excerpts, coming releases, sales, free books, cover reveals and more.

Check out our complete list of authors, too!

No spam, no junk. That's a promise!

Sign Up Here

www.dragonbladepublishing.com

Dearest Reader;

Thank you for your support of a small press. At Dragonblade Publishing, we strive to bring you the highest quality Historical Romance from some of the best authors in the business. Without your support, there is no 'us', so we sincerely hope you adore these stories and find some new favorite authors along the way.

Happy Reading!

CEO, Dragonblade Publishing

Additional Dragonblade books by Author Cerise Deland

Scarlett Affairs Series
Lord Ashley's Beautiful Alibi (Book 1)
Lord Ramsey's Red-Headed Ruin (Book 2)
Lord Appleby's Gorgeous Imposter (Book 3)
Lord Fournier's Shameless Princess (Book 4)

Matrimony! Series
If I Loved You (Book 1)
Because of You (Book 2)
You Made Me Love You (Book 3)

Naughty Ladies Series
Lady, Be Wanton (Book 1)
Lady, Behave (Book 2)
Lady, No More (Book 3)
Lady, You're Mine (Book 4, Novella)

The Lyon's Den Series
The Lyon's Share
The Lyon's Perfect Mate

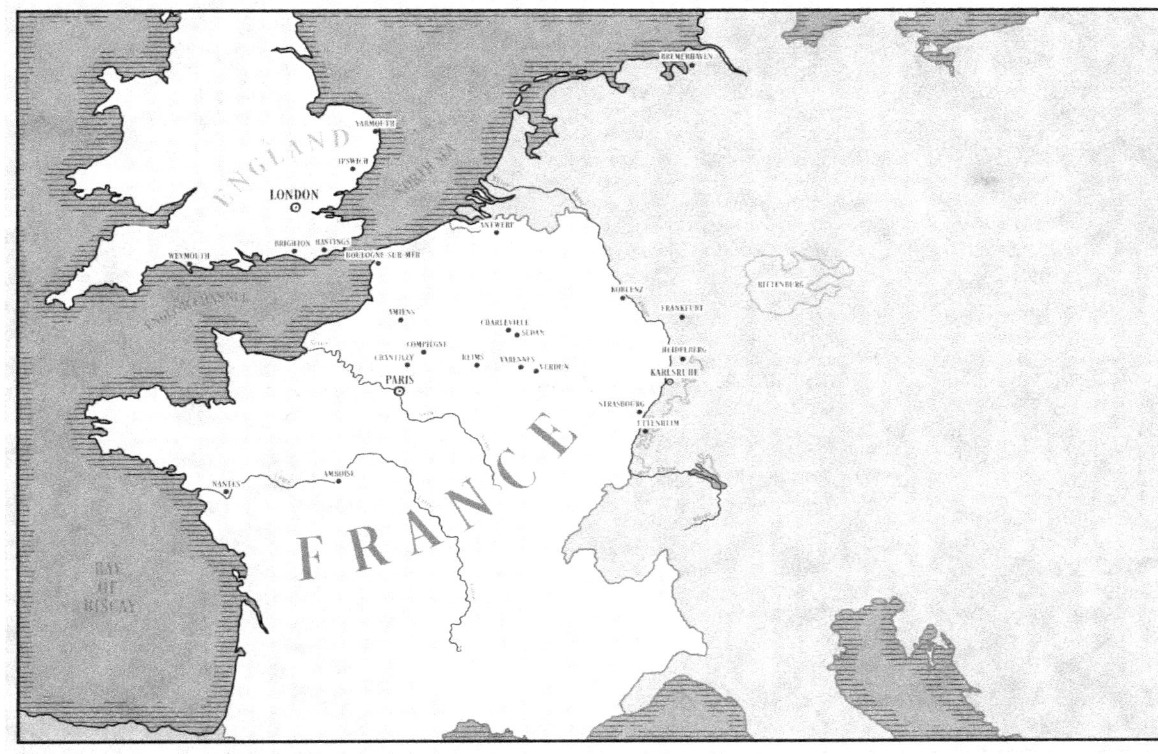

ENGLAND
NORTH SEA
ENGLISH CHANNEL
BAY OF BISCAY
FRANCE
LONDON
YARMOUTH
IPSWICH
BRIGHTON
HASTINGS
WEYMOUTH
BOULOGNE SUR MER
ANTWERP
BREMERHAVEN
KOBLENZ
FRANKFURT
HEIDELBERG
KARLSRUHE
RETTENBERG
AMIENS
CHARLEVILLE
SEDAN
COMPIEGNE
CHANTILLY
REIMS
VARENNES
VERDUN
PARIS
STRASBOURG
ETTENHEIM
NANTES
AMBOISE

Our heroine, Elizabeth—or Liesel, as she prefers to be called by her friends—is a crown princess of a very well positioned principality in the Holy Roman Empire. She is not only lovely and well educated, but hails from a rich city-state. Exactly like so many young ladies in German states at this time, she is afraid. She can flee the French into Russia, Prussia, or Vienna. But by the time Bonaparte abducts the Duke d'Enghien, that man has shown he cannot quell the advances of the French.

Liesel's home, the city-state of Rittenburg, I made up. But it is based on the real princely house of Thurn und Taxis. In 1615, they became the Imperial Postmasters of the Holy Roman Empire and while setting postal rates for most of Europe, became fabulously rich. (They continued in this role until 1867. Look them up! The family still have their titles and live in their magnificent castle.)

Liesel's intended fate to marry into the British royal family is not far from reality. Our Lisel has enough prestige, power and money and influence that the British Georgians want her in their family. She is not the only German royal desired by the British royal family.

George III and Queen Charlotte had 15 children. Of them, ten married and eight of them married royalty from the Germanic principalities. Often relatives married very close relatives. The list is long:

Prussia

Brunswick

Saxe-Meiningen

Wurttemberg

Saxe-Cobourg-Saalfeld

Hesse-Homburg

Hesse-Kassel

Mecklenburg-Strelitz

Most of these German territories abutted the German state of Hanover. Many were wealthy territories, like Baden and Württemberg. Others were small with little income but many royal progeny from which the Hanoverian rulers of Britain could choose potential spouses. Indeed, they were so numerous and often interbred—even before Victoria married her cousin Albert—that they suffered from all kinds of health ailments. But what these marriages with Germanic princes and princesses offered Britain was a sense of stability in a period when the post-Napoleonic Europeans wished for it most avidly.

What else is true in PRINCESS? The timing of Bonaparte being declared emperor for life and his relentless march to overtake the Continent. The race by many German leaders to leave the Continent before he could capture them. The alliance of many, like the Margrave of Baden, with Bonaparte. The crossing of General Caulaincourt over the Rhine to capture the unlucky and unwise Duke d'Enghien. The attempt by many to persuade that young Bourbon to leave Ettenheim. The outrage by Britain and Russia that the French violated international boundaries to be so bold as to capture, try and assassinate a prince of the Bourbon blood.

But now Dirk and Liesel live in peace until Clive, Lord Carlisle, calls upon both of them to discuss a mysterious lady who lives far too close—and is becoming far too dear.

Chapter One

10 Frederickstrasse
Karlsruhe, Margravate of Baden
June 10, 1803

S HE HAD FOUR words to say to this man tonight. Four. She would do the work he could not, had not. Why and how his mission was unfinished did not concern her. She was charged with the completion of this and she would see it done.

Her hired traveling carriage with good fittings and four fine horses covered the last miles from Ettenheim to Karlsruhe with speed. If comfort were rather lacking, and she bounced along the rough road that her distant cousin the Margrave of Baden had not cleared well despite his excellent funds from Bonaparte, she endured.

She huffed and buried her fingers in the thick wool coach blanket. She disliked riding at night, when the chill of the evening invaded her bones. Born in August in the tiny town of Leghorn Italy, she preferred heat. Any kind of heat.

Tonight, she'd give a blast of it to the man she called upon. She cared not for his reputation. Rather, his reputations, plural. An English baron, he was by blood a German prince as well, though through too many delineations of the Bergenhaven line to have any claim to land or power. Only influence. Which he had frittered away in Britain in his youth, gambling and carousing.

Though he rarely seduced females, young or widowed, he had departed London one dark night because of a scandal with one.

He had taken up other, subtler pursuits. Some said they were dissolute. Most said they were clandestine. Whatever his pleasure, he had traveled everywhere from Jaffa to Naples to Berlin and back.

Finally, after many years of wandering among princes and sheiks, he had settled here in Karlsruhe, the capital of Baden, this last year. Supposedly, his purpose was to enjoy the camaraderie of his maternal extended family. London gossips said he devoted his days and nights to dining, dancing, and gambling.

Yet rumor declared he had learned his lesson with women and engaged in no affairs. Some said a man so attractive, so virile, must have a mistress. None was known. Debutantes, wives, widows, and even the notorious bemoaned the prudence of Diedrich Werner Maxim Fournier, eighteenth Baron Fournier of Fournier Park, Kent. He was, after all, irresistible.

He was said to merit that approbation by his shocking good looks. His height, six feet and more. His stark white-blond hair, silken, it was said, to the touch. His iridescent hazel eyes, hotly savage, an inherited trait from his warlike Norman ancestors, no doubt. His strength of body, built by long hours of wrestling and swordplay in his raucous years at Heidelberg. His strength of spirit, demanded of him by his illustrious half-German mother and inculcated within him by his devil-may-care English father.

Diedrich—Dirk to his friends—was the scion of his large, prestigious clan. Beloved by all in his family and praised endlessly by those in continental court circles for his breeding, his intimate relationships with European royalty, and British politics, *Der Baron* Diedrich Fournier was the ideal diplomat.

Except he wasn't. His reputation had forbidden those in the Foreign Office to offer him any role. They were too rigid. He was too impulsive, too nonchalant for their strict standards. Too ruined.

Liesel had heard those in the London declare it. They had

reports that Fournier did more than play in his mother's childhood home. Word was he had done honorable work. He had arranged and escorted aristocrats dispossessed of their titles and lands to escape the long arm of the greedy French first consul, Napoleon Bonaparte. Fournier had done so not only secretly, but at his own expense.

Yet to serve one valuable noble, one man very close to the toppled French throne, Fournier had failed. Repeatedly. Miserably. So Liesel now must step in to point out the error of his ways and advance herself to the job he should have accomplished long ago.

"*Prinzessin.*" Her groom opened her carriage door and pulled his brim in deference.

They had arrived at Fournier's house? She had not noticed. She'd been so exasperated, so determined to get her way with him.

She alighted. Handing her wool blanket to her man, she did not bother to button her pelisse or don her little toque. She hated hats. They always fell off her head anyway. Only her mother's lovely amethyst tiara had ever stayed on her heavy hair. The last she had heard, her older brother Rainer was not keeping it for any potential fiancée. No, he was selling it to fund his travels, persuading other German princes and dukes to fight Bonaparte's intrusion into their lives and lands. Rainer had achieved success keeping their own little principality free of the control of Paris.

Our family is safe and our subjects too. Not like the man I just left, who refuses to see reason.

Enough! She knew what to do here.

"I will remain only a few minutes," she told the groom *auf Deutsch*. Here in Baden, along the border with France, most spoke French as well as German. But each household chose its primary language. Rainer, despite his French and English education, had always kept to his homeland German, so Liesel kept to it as well.

On an exhale, she took the steps of the wide porch of the very fine-looking house. Four stories of pure white stucco with wooden trim of window casements, the house was a city mansion with a welcoming front door of a delightful chocolate. Fournier's residence, said to have been built by his great-grandfather when summoned to visit the Baden margrave and his family, stood on the corner of a wide, cobbled street. Gaslight flickered in the well-appointed street lamps. No dark, ugly corners offered thugs holes in which to hide. This little territory of the traitorous margrave was prosperous, filled with money given by Bonaparte and soldiers conscripted by him. No wonder no one walked the street. Nor did carriages idle here, either. People were home, wondering what their erstwhile margrave might decide to supply the French upstart with tomorrow.

Plus, it was late. Past dinner. Past time for schnapps and intimate conversations. The moon and stars above shone like sugared candies in the black velvet sky. Only a few lights flickered in the first- and second-floor windows of Fournier's house. Good. He was alone.

She'd lifted her hand to raise the huge brass lion knocker when the door fell open to her. She arched one brow. Her royal glare of intimidation worked well on everyone.

This butler, however, took a long, cool look at her, which included her lack of hat, gloves, and smile. He took his sweet, rude time. At the conclusion of his perusal, he smiled with tight efficiency.

"*Guten Abend, Fräulein,*" the butler said, and stepped aside to welcome her into the pristine, high-ceiled Baroque foyer. "*Warum sind Sie heir?*"

"I am Princess Elizabeth von Rittenburg." She kept to the German, since she had no knowledge of Fournier's house staff and their practices. "I am here to see Baron Fournier."

The butler's white bushy brows shot up. "*Mein Prinz ist nicht—*"

Fournier was going by his German princely title, was he? Big of him. Humility had never been his hallmark. She took a breath. "Bitte, inform your master I am here and I will speak with him immediately."

"As I began to tell you, *princess,* my master is not receiving at this hour."

"But I am here now and I will see him. Now, sir."

"Princess—"

"Where is he, sir?" She glanced up the main staircase. A light streamed from a room down the corridor. "At dinner?"

"No!"

She cocked an ear for the rhythms of the house. Footsteps sounded not on the next floor up, but higher. People spoke. Servants at their nightly duties? *Yes.*

She hoisted her skirts and took the grand staircase. Her fingers slid along the ornate mahogany balustrade, and she could not hide her appreciation. Though Fournier's house was in town, it resembled many larger, grand palaces with its intricate chandeliers and sconces and lavish gold trim upon the moldings. She was impressed—and distracted by the quiet air of serenity here. She increased her speed.

"Princess!" The man nipped at her heels. "You cannot go up!"

But I am, sir. I am. She rounded the landing and kept going. No lights, no sounds emanated from the rooms along the hall. So then. The man she sought was in his bedroom suite.

She hurried up the next flight, her pursuer not able to keep pace. At the landing of the second-floor stairs, she was rewarded with the bass notes of more voices. Louder. Men. Two of them. One bade his master good evening, and the next moment, she heard no sounds at all. Then came a splash of water.

Ah. Fournier was bathing? At this hour?

Fine. She rejoiced that he had such poor timing as to allow her knowledge of his whereabouts.

She found the suite, the old, handsome, carved door ajar. She sailed past a footman whose mouth dropped open. Then she pushed wide a boudoir door to find the man she wanted.

And oh my. Her heart stopped. Her mouth watered. From white-blond head past massive shoulders, rippled arms and sculpted trunk, admirable hips and very impressive masculine assets, Baron Diedrich Fournier was a delicious sight every woman should behold.

DIRK LIFTED ONE leg to sink into his tub, let out a breath, and…

A strange woman barged into his bathroom.

She halted at the door—and stared.

He gaped.

She blushed.

He scowled. *Who the hell is she that she—*

"Baron Fournier!"

She knew his name. Knew of him.

He spread one hand out in question. Of course he was Fournier. This was his house. His boudoir. His tub. *"Und Sie?"* he asked, as blasé as a naked man might when confronted by a woman he did not know.

She squeezed shut her blinking eyes. Her hair—a mass of gold rich as a Spanish conquistador's—fell in long waves over her slim shoulders.

He blinked. Came to his senses, enough to reach for the nearest thing. That, sadly, was the white serviette thrown over his dinner tray. A scrap of cloth. But he plastered it over his *accoutrements* and hoped that sufficed.

"Remove to my bedroom, *Fräulein*, and I will find more suitable means to—"

She glared at him. Fluttering her lashes, she fought to focus her eyes not on his genitals, covered—*weren't they?*—by his napkin, but on his eyes. She failed. Then she whirled around— and for half a second, he thought she would run out as fast as she'd rushed in.

But no. She went to slam the door shut in his butler's face. Then she twisted the key in the lock. And pocketed the damn thing.

Wonderful. I am to be ravished?

Then she swished her skirts as she rounded on him once more.

Gad. What a hellion! What had he done to rile this desperate beauty?

"*Fräulein, bitte—*"

"I am Elizabeth von Rittenburg."

What? Rittenburg? His mind bounced along in her German, his English. Rainer's sister? What in the hell was she doing here? *In my house? At this hour of the night?* "Pardon me, princess, I—"

She extended an arm, pointed a finger at his…

Hmm. Yes. He got the point. But he had few choices to protect his modesty, didn't he?

"You have failed."

To cover myself? He did not bother to look. This was most likely true. He glanced around for something bigger than the napkin he currently wore.

"Failed, baron! And I am here—"

"Uninvited, *Fräulein.* Go to the other room while I—"

"No."

He rolled his eyes. "It is an ungodly hour, *Fräulein.* And I am rather indisposed."

She stamped her foot.

Three years old, was she?

"You failed!" she accused him, her cheeks pink, her fists curled.

"At…?"

"The Duke of Enghien. You were to get him out of Baden. Hide him away. Make it impossible for Bonaparte to harass him."

He stiffened. Who was she? How did she know that? Was she a French agent?

He knew them all in this territory. It was his business to know and keep track. But of Enghien, the Bourbon heir to the French throne, he knew much. He had visited with the fellow, often in fact, but it was all done under cover of frivolity. *Fräu-lein—*"

"You will address me as 'princess' or 'Your Highness,'" she scolded him, and in good English, too. Elizabeth, the famous, the *infamous* lady who was engaged to a decrepit Hanoverian and had refused to marry him because of his body odor and drunken stupors. Elizabeth—Liesel—Rainer's younger sister, whom the man adored. What in hell was she doing in Baden? Wasn't she pouring tea in London, outraging the *ton* and looking to catch a good husband Rainer would approve of?

"Very well. Princess." He flexed his shoulders. He had to get his foot out of this tub and his jolly roger suitably protected from this harpy. "Please, if you will turn your back."

She blanched. But she also refused to look away. Her gaze kept dropping to the important items on his body. *I guess curiosity killed all the good in those girls' etiquette classes, eh?*

He pointed toward towels piled atop a nearby footstool. "If you will please move, princess, I can avail myself of cover and we can discuss this like civilized—"

"Discuss?" She sashayed forward. "Is that all you do, baron? Discuss? I will not fall to your tactics. You do not know how to *discuss.* You fail to *persuade.* You fail to move him and—"

"Princess," Dirk sighed. He'd had this conversation with Enghien himself. Too often. Dirk had no idea how she considered herself the designated person to save the Bourbon heir to the French throne. But God bless her. She would find the fellow as immovable as he had. "Enghien is a man in love."

She frowned. "What?"

"In love." Dirk had a few facts to impart. "He wishes to marry a lady. That woman flirts and parries. He lives for her smiles."

"He will die for them, too, if he does not flee!"

"I quite agree."

"And still, you have not persuaded him."

"Princess, I beg you—"

She took a step forward. And another. Her nearness nearly

sent him to his knees. Her eyes were a royal shade of purple. Her lips were supple and pink, her complexion perfect cream. She was a rainbow of color that defined her exquisite face and led him to note the elegant arc of her shoulders and the heaving swell of her décolleté. Hell hath no fury like a woman angered, but he'd rarely met one. None so bold as to barge into his bath. Nor so wild as to insult him, and hold him at her mercy, in his bare skin.

A laugh of delight and outrage burst from him. He was smitten.

She ground her teeth and came closer. "Listen to me, Fournier."

Oh, you do have me.

"I am now in charge of Enghien."

"Absurd." *How very beautiful you are. Rainer never told me.*

"Not so, sir."

He had the patience of Job. That was one characteristic that suited him well in his work. This gorgeous creature might charm him to his core, but she had scorched his tolerance with her fire. "First, princess, you assume I was in charge. Secondly, whatever authority gave you such a mission—"

"Do not trifle with me!"

He took a step forward, and two more. The napkin drifted to the floor. She stood her ground, but he'd expected that. He'd have her no other way. Ripe with righteousness and rigor, she was a woman few would want and few others would dare to rival. He was one of those few, on both counts. She did not know it. He'd never tell her. But she challenged him, as few women could. Or did.

More, she set his body burning…and he grinned like the rogue he was reputed to be. "I invite you to amuse me, princess. Since you assume my role in the poor duke's reluctance to leave Baden, I will likewise assume you have some ripe hold over him that I cannot claim, eh? What could that be, hmm?"

The implication of scandalous behavior on her part fell like stones on her. "How dare you, sir! I have been put in charge of him by the Foreign Office."

Those twits. "How good of them."

"They want him gone to London."

"Really?" Dirk would have crossed his arms, but, of course, he liked facing her in as raw a manner as she did him. So he stood in his natural state, his height affording him the ability to hover over his intruder.

She did not cower.

But if she glanced down, she could note evidence of his growing interest. He was certain she wanted him to recoil or at least agree, anything but argue—or find her desirable. "They can want all they want, my dear princess, but Enghien will not leave."

"I will do it."

He scoffed. "Then you are a better man than I."

He did cross his arms then, even though he knew he provoked her. But damn! *She barged in on me! Let her look, by God. Her price to pay, not mine.*

Elizabeth of Rittenburg shook her head, and in the move, her gaze swept his biceps, his hips, and more. She gulped, then blushed from her slender throat to her cheeks. His male interest in her, despite her outrageous behavior, was there for her to see.

He was flattered at her reaction. But also done with this contretemps. Silently cursing, he bent to grab a towel.

She took one step back, but squared her shoulders. "I have come to notify you that you are not to see the duke any longer. You have failed, sir. Failed terribly. The duke's life is in danger now. I am in charge and I will see this thing done."

At that, she spun away. In a flounce of apple-green silken skirts and midnight-blue wool coat, she tossed her golden, unbound tresses—and left him where he stood.

But fie on him! She would not have the last word.

He slung the towel around his waist, knotted the thing, and strode after her. His bare feet met bedroom rug and hall carpet, but the slick marble stairs had him slipping. He flapped along, clinging to the railings like a weakling.

"Wait!" he yelled after her.

But she kept going.

He picked up his pace but slid as if he were skating. *It will serve her right if I fall at her feet!*

"Wait!" *By God!*

He rounded the last landing, spied his man Bartel at the door and a man and woman staring up at him—plus the princess, who waved a dismissive hand at him.

He yelled at her anyway. "You cannot go! You must tell me the details!"

She whirled. Her smile was one of triumph. "You failed! Go home!"

Then she flew off into the dark night, taking all her shimmering fireworks with her.

Dirk halted. The explosions the woman created had swept through his house and his life and left him…undone.

He had failed. That was true. But how had she known? Had one of his runners to Scarlett Hawthorne been caught? Had one of his messages been decoded? Or had Scarlett and the Foreign Office shared intelligence? Bloody hell, none of that seemed probable. He now had to pick apart any cracks in his network back to London. Not a happy job, but necessary. Meanwhile, his lovely Princess of the Night took over as Enghien's nursemaid.

Well, heaven had better help her. The duke was not inclined to agree. Another example of how love destroyed people's good common sense. Dirk dared hope that Enghien's love for his lady was not to be the destruction of more than that.

But all that was for tomorrow to fix.

Here now, below him in his foyer, were two people who had witnessed this altercation. Visitors. One he knew—a dear old friend, Tate Cantrell, Earl of Appleby—and some lovely, petite blonde, whom he did not know.

"Appleby," he hailed his friend of many years with affection. The earl and his lady friend looked as if they needed a meal, a bath, a good bed…and rest.

Dirk would give them all of it. Tate would not be here at such an hour with his friend if circumstances did not demand it. He needed help, and Dirk could provide it. Was that not his sole occupation in this world?

He grimaced at his condition. "If you will excuse me a few minutes, I will have my man Bartel welcome you properly. I will join you both soon. Now, if you please…" And he spun one hand in a circle, hoping they would turn away from his extraordinary display.

IT WAS NOT until two or three in the morning that he managed to fall asleep. He had obsessed about the shocking appearance of the beguiling Princess of Rittenburg.

Liesel, as she was fondly known by her family and friends, was the second eldest of five children of the recently deceased Prince Gerhard von Rittenburg. She was known throughout the Continent as a firebrand, the beauty of the family, and the one sent to London seven years ago, at age fifteen, to marry a cousin of King George III. She never had. The reasons were described in detail in every gossip rag from London to St. Petersburg. In fact, the sheets gleefully hit upon each refusal, each slight that pretty Liesel had given for her failure to post at any church.

Dirk shook his head. The Princess of Rittenburg, it was rumored, had taken one look three years ago at the dyspeptic, overweight Charles Edward Stuart—the third Duke of Isenhurst, cousin to King George of Britain—tossed her mane of glorious hair, and marched away. Court gossip had it that she had gone straight from her engagement ceremony to her aged nurse in London and told that lady to return home to Gerhard. Liesel had then written to her father, demanded he hand over her allowance, and taken over the house he leased for her in Hanover Square. She joined the fashionable leadership of the *haute ton,* went about her shopping and dancing with a lady's companion only two years older than her. She was also said to have told her father she would marry if and when she found a man worthy of her.

Last autumn, she'd disappeared. Rumor had it she had sailed to the new United States. Others said she'd run off with her butler. But Dirk now knew what she'd done. She'd volunteered her services to those fools in the Foreign Office, who obviously believed she might help them pry Enghien from his little house in Ettenheim, a tiring ride of sixty miles to the south of Karlsruhe.

Clearly, Elizabeth von Rittenburg had her talents. The lovely princess spoke English, French, German, and Italian. She had been educated in the finest Geneva school for ladies of royal class, then polished off by the dry standards of the British in a dreary little young ladies' academy in Kent. Dirk knew of Liesel's arrival there because his own mother had met the poor girl.

"Bedeviled," his mama had described the princess. "Imagine, being made to marry that hideous old Stuart. She is quite pretty and spirited—and she will shrivel to dust closeted with him."

That last, Dirk knew, would never be true. The lady did not shrivel, nor shrink, nor would she ever closet herself with any soul whom she did not grace with all her favors. He closed his eyes, remembering her fire and her virginal reaction to the scene she had precipitated. Liesel of Rittenburg was a prize for any man of standing and wealth. She was a princess, meant to wed a prince. Few of those might still have the means or the prestige to be her equal. Bonaparte had destroyed so many nobles on the Continent. But her looks, her wit, and her pedigree made her a woman any man would want on his arm as his wife.

Still, few would take her. Not now that she'd defied the Hanovers and her father. She was known as a hellion, and if anyone learned she worked for the Foreign Office, she would be an outcast. Women did not *do* such work. Not even princesses with bloodlines, wealth, and pluck.

But what a woman Elizabeth of Rittenburg was. She was wise

to have refused to marry the royal cousin. Being chained to another for life and having no say in the choice was a travail from which Dirk himself had rebelled. It was the very reason he spent his life mostly abroad. Away from the mother he adored. Even now that his father lay in his grave in the family mausoleum, Dirk remained apart from whom and what he loved. Instead, he performed the work so necessary to the independence of Britain.

"And now we have this," he said to himself.

A lady on a mission. Sent to supplant him.

But why now? What did she know that he did not? And what was he to do now…except learn if she had the ability to persuade the young Bourbon heir to the defunct throne of France to leave his home five miles from the Rhine and the French border?

"And she'd better hurry, too," he murmured to himself.

Because Bonaparte had put out a new diplomatic attempt to persuade more German princes to come to his side and part with Vienna. The Holy Roman Emperor, Francis, was in a fit.

Did daring Liesel know that? Because if Bonaparte succeeded and persuaded those princes whose territories surrounded her brother Rainer's to accede to his hegemony, then he would order all who did not agree to abdicate. Or perhaps do away with them altogether.

Dirk punched his pillows and lay down in his bed. As he stared up at the canopy over his head, he saw her regal spirit, her incomparable fire—and wished her well.

But Liesel, lovely woman. You might be charged with saving the Bourbon Duke of Enghien, but you should instead apply yourself to saving your siblings—and your own flawless skin.

Chapter Two

10 Frederickstrasse
Karlsruhe, Baden
March 12, 1804

L IESEL SLID FROM her poor horse's back, looped the reins over the front hitch, and climbed the broad portico steps of Baron Fournier's grand stone and timber mansion. She was bone tired. Cold to the bone, too. Worse, she was a dirty mess in her male riding coat and dusty Hessians, but she had no choice about her sad appearance. No choice about what she had to do.

She picked up the lion's head knocker and let it bang on Fournier's front door. It took her two more appeals to get his man to answer.

"Prinzessin!" Fournier's aged butler remembered Liesel, his wild white brows high with surprise. It was gratifying, if embarrassing, and it eliminated so much explanation of who she was. He most likely thought her here to upbraid his master again. Far from it.

"Please, sir. I need to see Baron Fournier." She saw his dismay at her appearance. Worse, he frowned, looking down his long, lean nose at her. He recalled how rash she'd been months ago when she had barged in and taken the house by storm—and confronted his master, naked at his bath. "I will be good. I have come a long way. Please."

He peered over her shoulder and saw her steed, the mare's head hanging, exhausted from her frantic ride.

"*Javohl*, do come in." He examined her sorry state and, from his frown, found nothing new to like. Especially not her leather riding breeches that fit her like new skin. But he did welcome her inside. "*Mein Herr* is not here."

"May I wait? It is most important. A matter of life and death, truly." Out of a tinge of guilt and need, she had to add, "I do apologize for my rudeness when I was here last."

The butler's aquiline features did the impossible and softened. "*Princessin*, might you like food, drink…or perhaps a bath?"

The last word had her blinking at him to kill the surprise at his acceptance. She'd expected his hauteur, not his kindness. "*Ja, bitte*. And care for my horse."

"*Natürlich*." He arched a brow and gave her a ghost of a smile. "Tea? Soup?" he asked.

"Whatever Cook has in the kitchen at this hour will please me. *Danke schön*."

He spread his hands wide. "Your cape, princess?"

She picked at the fingertips of her worn leather gloves, then surrendered them with her old tri-collared coat—happy to get rid of the thing, actually. She'd worn it the past few weeks because it was wool, warm, and serviceable as part of her disguise. She'd bought it from a farrier in Ettenheim from whom she usually hired horses. Now, she did not need it. Her masquerade, like her mission, was at an end. She was here because she needed not just a new cloak, but new clothes and, most of all, a new friend. Would that Lord Fournier could forgive her rash behavior of months ago and become that necessary ally. If he did not, she knew no other in Baden to ask. Two of her best friends in Ettenheim had gone missing lately, and…

She swallowed against her horror of what had most likely happened to them.

"Come this way." The butler curled her coat over his arm and sniffed at the appearance of her waistcoat and shirt sleeves. Her casual male attire affronted the servant, but riding alone for miles to get here tonight had nothing to do with formality.

She had urgent business here, so she brushed off his criticism. She followed him up the magnificent staircase, which she had not taken much time to admire previously. Up they trod to the first floor and down the wide, ivory-painted hall so gilded in gold leaf that her tired eyes burned. She did not remember the beauty of this house. The tranquility, either. She breathed it in. How she welcomed it after the chaos she had witnessed. She followed silently and in wonder, like a child who goes to the village square in hopes of mummers and magicians and toffee candies to make life sweeter.

"*Bitte,* please be comfortable, princess." Fournier's butler stood aside and indicated the settee across the room. The walls were a deep forest green, the furniture opulent swirls of gold-painted wood, while the upholstery contrasted in bright yellow Chinoiserie. Here was quiet and repose. "I will return with refreshments, and send Lord Fournier to you as soon as he arrives home."

"*Danke schön,* Herr…?" She wished to observe all the rules of etiquette this night. Gratitude and polite regard were the first she should employ.

"Bartel, princess."

"Thank you, Herr Bartel." Then she sank down onto the most comfortable chair she'd known in weeks. In warmth and safety, she gladly waited in the enchanting home of the man she had insulted and shamed not so long ago.

DIRK HAD HAD a long journey, endless in distance as well as heartache. What he'd seen last night in Offenburg, forty miles to the south, angered him. Frightened him, too. But affairs were beyond him now. He could not save the young heir to the

Bourbon throne who lived in the small town of Ettenheim sixty miles south.

The Duke of Enghien's refusal of Dirk's help to leave Baden defied reason. Or rather, most reason. Only one had kept him tied to his home these past three years—his charming wife. The love of his life, Charlotte de Rohan, also adored her house, her family and friends. The young Duke of Enghien humored her and would not leave.

"He may also do it at the cost of his life."

"*Mein Herr?*" His stableman to whom he handed the reins of his mount questioned his ramblings.

"Talking to myself, Braun. I must, to keep my sanity. Excuse me." He peered through the shadows in his dimly lit stables. "Whose horse is that? Do we have a visitor?"

"*Ja, Mein Herr.* A young lady came an hour ago. Her horse is almost lame with the hard ride she asked of him."

Dirk walked over to the next stall and ran a hand down the horse's long, tangled mane. The animal, a mix of Arabian and some other, snuffled at the caress. He could think of few ladies who would come to him all of a sudden, riding a horse so near the end of its stamina. Only one woman came to mind as a lady who might call on him in desperation. His blood burned to think Liesel of Rittenburg would come to him once more—and tonight of all nights—seeking solace. "Not to worry, my friend," he crooned to the horse. "Braun will see you thorough this."

His staff were stout-hearted folk who served him faithfully. With what he had seen this day in Offenburg, he would soon have to dismiss them all. They would be at the mercy of their margrave, that slippery fellow who had aligned himself with Bonaparte last year and put his own people under the burden of tax and conscription for the French first consul. Dirk had long predicted it would come to this, after Enghien proclaimed himself secure and cited the border between Baden and eastern France as the barrier to invasion. But the border was porous, made of the River Rhine. A good boat—even a sturdy pontoon in dry season—would serve an adventurous Frenchman to cross quickly. To hell with diplomatically sacred borders. What was sacred to Bonaparte?

Only his own neck.

Dirk took the yard from his stables to his kitchen door. Yesterday, he had seen Bonaparte's close friend and general leave the city of Strasbourg, France with more than three hundred French dragoons and a detachment of gendarmerie at night. The party of perhaps a thousand armed men headed across the Rhine for Offenburg, Baden. That friend of Bonaparte's, General Armand Caulaincourt, rarely left the Little Corporal's side, usually only for secret personal missions. For him to leave Paris and come to Baden boded only ill. Dirk feared what ill that was. They'd come to harass Enghien. Or worse.

He flung wide the kitchen door and bade the surprised cook and kitchen maids a good evening.

"All is well," he assured them with a wave and the small smile he could muster. It would have to suffice. What they did not know about the French intrusion into their margrave's territory would not worry them.

Only when I begin my preparations to leave for England will they seek the cause and begin to fret.

He turned for the servants' stairway. He was two steps up when a man's voice beckoned him from below. He swung around.

"Bartel. Forgive my entering by the back door. Braun tells me we have a visitor?"

"*Javohl.* It is Princess von Rittenburg. I have placed her in the green salon, Mein Herr."

"Well, well. She barges in once more. Plus I need a bath, too!" He could find irony in her appearance, even if Bartel saw none. Still, for a man who had a reputation as a rake, Dirk had limits to how frankly and often a woman might show her interest in him.

But his mind filled with reasons why she'd come to him.

What does she know about what occurs in the south?

"*Mein baron...*"

"What is wrong?" His butler looked flustered. "Is she demanding?"

"No, sir. She is in a very sad state."

Dirk's first thought ran through him like an alarm bell. "Is she hurt?"

"No, sir. But she is pale, tired, unkempt, and wearing men's clothing."

Running from something or someone. Or to *me? This time for help.* If she had any indication of what he'd seen last night, beautiful Liesel was here to seek refuge or help. This time, he doubted she wished to rant and rave at him. Far from it. If she knew what happened south of them, she needed his assistance. Perhaps more.

Bartel joined him on the stairs. "I have provided food and wine, sir. She needed it badly."

Dirk handed over his hat and cloak. "Good. I'm in no condition to receive her at once. My ride was long. But do tell her I will go to her in a few minutes. Did she indicate what she wished to discuss?"

"Not a word, sir."

She saves her news. I do not blame her. Those throughout Baden will be frightened by it. "I will ask for a hot bath before I see her, Bartel. Don't bother to call for Otto. I will not need a valet tonight. I will be quick. Tell her I will be down in ten minutes."

Fear ticked through his veins. What had Liesel seen or learned? The lady had her own reputation as one who was in command of herself. No other lady had ever stood up to Queen Charlotte of Great Britain and refused to marry one of her cousins because she did not like his bodily habits. Even more scandalously, she had proceeded to live her life in Society as a free lady, until about two years ago, when she had simply disappeared from the *ton. Only to appear on my doorstep last year.*

Now she is here once more.

According to rumor, since last June, she had been seen in Strasbourg, Berlin, and even Vienna. Dirk had not seen her since she last appeared in his boudoir. But now she needed him, at least for an urgent discussion. Whatever her problems, a woman chased was a woman who needed help and even comfort. Dirk would provide both. That was his mission for so many along the Rhine these past months. But more than that, she was the sister to one of his best friends—and Dirk would move heaven and earth to aid her.

In his suite, he stripped off his riding clothes. A shambles, they were. Fit only for burning. Two footmen came with bathwater, and he submerged himself and washed quickly. His mind whirled with what Liesel knew, and he worried where she had been.

Dirk hoped she knew nothing of Caulaincourt and the French. He would say nothing to Bartel. If that was her news, he'd ask her not to reveal anything to his staff. He wished to minimize his servants' alarm about the French contingent until he had them organized, all house weapons cleaned and ammunition ready.

His household and groomsmen were hardy Germans of kind heart and good minds. But if the Margrave of Baden knew that the French had invaded his territory of Offenburg forty miles south—if that ruler had even secretly permitted the French access to his domain—would not that man also allow them to march north and accost the last British citizen who remained in his capital? For if they took Dirk, he had no doubts the French had no compunction about attacking anyone who tried to prevent them from taking him away. That meant his loyal servants. And he would not have them pay that price.

Now, here in his house, he also had the honor of hosting the headstrong beauty who'd once more arrived at his house at the most inauspicious moment. He'd hear her out, but he had suspicions that what she required of him was more than supper. What he owed her was more than succor. He would not allow the French to seize her either.

Unnerved, Dirk emerged from his rooms. Refreshed bodily as much as he could be, he was presentable. Yet his whole being burned because he knew his lovely visitor was at risk, too.

Bartel awaited him at the landing.

Dirk followed him down the long hall to the main salon. "*Danke schön*, Bartel. I wish not to disturb the rhythm of the house more than I have."

Dirk turned away, flames of anger at the French licking at him. What he had seen in Offenburg had sealed the fate of those who lived in his beloved grandmother's province.

Now, everywhere, there would be war.

And his visitor was one he had to save from its horrors.

Chapter Three

D IRK WALKED THROUGH the salon doors just as his caller sighed and set her half-filled plate on the small table before her. She rose to greet him, the look of a startled animal suffusing her lovely oval face. Her polite homage of standing to greet him was totally unnecessary, especially at this time of night in what was obviously an emergency for her.

"Princess, I welcome you," he said with a polite bow as she rose to her feet.

She was dressed in breeches, boots, and a faded blue man's waistcoat, gaping over a fine muslin shirt clinging to her curves. Wherever she'd come from, she had ridden hard and fast. Mud spattered her boots. One small splash marred her left cheek. Her hair had suffered in her run. Yet its gold blinded him as it had the first night he had beheld her.

She'd acted a right hellion to him months ago, but now, clearly, in her anxious state, she was more subdued. And from what he and Bartel had gathered, she'd come alone, too. Hazardous for a woman to be out in the world without a soul to call her friend, no matter her hauteur or her knowledge of the terrain. For that, he took to her more kindly than ever before. She was his friend's sister, and he would help her.

"I do apologize for my delay." He owed her that. He could

tell from her expression and her anxious stance that she was not here to scold him. A relief, that. They could move to the matter that obsessed her.

She tried to smile. The effort was valiant, but her attempt failed. "Your man said you were expected, my lord. I asked to wait and hope you do not find it remiss that I was so forward."

Tonight she was civil. He welcomed it. He himself was tired and dismayed by what he'd learned today. He was in no mood to argue or fend off the level of frustration she had presented to him in June. Tonight, she was a woman undone, fatigued and needy.

"Not at all forward of you." He strode forward, drawn to her like a bee to flower. Water to land. Moon to earth. He'd been captivated by her beauty months ago, even though she was so furious with him. Yet he gazed at her now, and his heart swelled just to see her so bereft, so unkempt…and yet so exquisite.

He grabbed the back of chair—that or he'd fail to find words. Only to himself could he admit one thing: she had lived in his reverie, lo, these many months, as the loveliest woman he had ever seen. Yet he was a wise man, raised by caring parents, educated well, and tempered by a Society that condemned him for a transgression he had not committed. He was thirty-one years of age, and he was wise to the effects of a lovely woman on a man. Especially one so long celibate as he. Beauty might not commend a lady to a man and forgive all else, but he knew Liesel's past, and her reputation made her even more appealing to him. She had courage and stamina, a mind of her own, all characteristics that commended any man or woman.

If he were known as more honorable, if he were of higher rank than mere baron, if he and she lived in less perilous times and she were not a princess of one of the richest principalities in Europe, he could warm to her, want her, keep her as his own. But he was none of those, and she was beyond his reach. He would maintain his distance—and aid her in all she required.

She tipped her head, modest and sweet. "I am grateful for your hospitality, sir."

He smiled at her. Her English was so smooth that he would not have known she'd been born in Rittenburg and belonged to one of the most ancient royal families of Europe. Her six years in a Kent school had polished a continental jewel into a rare gem that those in George III's court had once coveted as one of their own.

Dirk could barely breathe looking at her. Never had he viewed a woman of such grace and perfection. He'd been struck by her that night she invaded his boudoir. God knew, he probably marveled at her now like a fifteen-year-old boy. She shimmered, so near, so ethereal in the candlelight. Even in her threadbare clothes that fell over her svelte body like a waterfall, she was delectable.

Better, tonight, she was not angry with him. Worse, she was distraught. That she did not hide. The lines of her oval face drew tight against her cheeks. Her extraordinary violet eyes were wide with expectation. Her lips, lush and pink, were pursed. Her hands, her elegant, ringless fingers, clasped tightly together. And her stance, regal though it appeared, defined the insecurities of her presence here.

"I deserve no apologies, Lord Fournier. I am the one who intrudes. And just as I did last time I was here, I come at a terrible hour."

He reached out and took her hands between his. She was cold. Trembling. One did not touch a princess of the blood. But tonight, at this moment, he cared not for protocol. His job was to soothe her and welcome her. She was a guest, seeking relief. In his firm embrace, he felt her muscles relax. "Let us speak no more of our last meeting, Your Highness. I see you are distressed, and I bid you to calm yourself and tell me at once how I can help you."

He led her to sit on the settee beside him—so close, he ordered himself to listen to her, lest he simply admire her and drink in her loveliness. But he had such problems. Unlike that time before, he could now regard her at his leisure, and oh, did he enjoy the ambiance.

Last year, the moment she had spoken to him, she had arrested him. His sight, his hearing, his masculine appreciation for her elegant female form were captured by her outrage—and her grasp of power. Of course, it was of some consequence that he had been naked, and she, though fiercely angry with him, took little notice. But now, she presented a problem, a wound. She wanted help. He was not surprised, because tonight, even before she arrived, he had garnered his own evidence that she had failed at her task. She was as finished as he, failing at the same mission he had set more than a year and half ago.

"I have just come from Ettenheim." Her voice in its normal octave was melodic, a contralto full of mellow enticements.

"Ah." This was indeed the worst. How much did she know about the French invasion of Baden territory? "Tell me all you know."

"The Duke of Enghien knows that Bonaparte's Foreign Affairs Minister Talleyrand and Chief of Police Fouché have declared Bonaparte's life in danger. They think Enghien plots to lead a coup, enter France, and kill him. I saw Enghien this morning and told him he must leave at once, sail north along the Rhine, or go south to Lake Constance—simply do *something*!"

Dirk nodded, resigned to the inevitable now. "He refuses."

"You know?" she asked with sinking voice and shadowed gaze. Clearly, Liesel of Rittenburg was not yet resigned to the dismal future the duke had sealed for himself.

"I do." Dirk pondered how much to reveal to her. Those in Scarlett's ring had rules of conduct, all meant to keep each of them safe should one be taken and tortured for information. She had divined his real purpose with Enghien and told him of hers. Both their lives were at risk. Still, he would tread carefully, offering little. "I fear the duke has run out of time."

"I told him not to go to Strasbourg last month," she bit off in frustration, and then looked miserable for having ridiculed the man.

"That is not the greatest of his so-called sins." He got to his feet and went to the sideboard, where Bartel had furnished the long bar with an array of cold foods, brandy, schnapps, and a crystal carafe of white wine plunged in a bucket of ice. "Forgive me, I have been on the road all day. I have not eaten, and I must."

He'd noticed that she had partaken of only a bit of Bartel's offerings. She must have more. Why a young woman of the old German aristocracy needed a fine meal, a tall brandy, and a good night's sleep was a nightmare. That was of Bonaparte's making. "Will you join me, Your Highness, in wine, brandy, or schnapps, perhaps?"

"Schnapps, please."

He smiled to himself. The lady was no wilting flower. He poured and returned to her with a full goblet of peach liquor for both of them. "The French know that the duke has received a pension from the British government for many years. It was the means by which he survived."

She huffed as she took her glass. "Heaven knows that neither of Louis XVI's two surviving brothers sent him anything to live on."

The self-styled King of France, Louis XVIII, who lived in Prussia these days, and his younger brother Artois were miserly pimps, living off the charity of continental royalty who would host them and clutching every amenity to their own breasts.

"They are two greedy buggers." Dirk sat beside her and took a sip of his schnapps. The warmth of it sliding down his throat increased his good humor, and he took another drink. "But when their cousin the Duke of Enghien refused to renounce the throne last March, Bonaparte knew he would always be a threat. Marrying the Rohan girl and living in her family's house helped the duke to live a happy life."

Dirk watched her closely to see her reaction to his next statement. She did not stir, only meeting his stark gaze with her own.

"But he has welcomed too many French monarchists to his home. Agents have warned him to be less hospitable. Plus, he puts his person in danger. He remained much too near the border, and the French fear he can easily cross…and bring an army."

She drank, taking her time to savor the liquor and close her eyes in appreciation. Dirk's masculine interest stirred far too much at the look of satisfaction on her face. This was no time to allow his libido to rise. He cleared his throat and focused on her earnestness instead.

She opened her eyes. "He is peaceful. Married. In love with his wife," she added. "He has no guards, no army. But today, he received a runner who told of a detachment of soldiers crossing the Rhine. A general led them."

Caulaincourt. Yes, I saw him myself. Dirk had met the man two years ago when he arrived in Paris with his cousin and head of mission, Kane, Lord Ashley. He would not alarm her more by revealing any of that. Instead, he gave what little comfort he could. "It is a breach of international law to cross a border armed."

"Yes!" She waved a hand. "But what does my cousin, the margrave, who calls himself a benevolent ruler—what does he care? He has aligned himself with Bonaparte over and over again. Karl of Baden wants more land and a ducal title. He petitioned Vienna to name him an independent elector in the empire. I don't believe he has any desire to stop a contingent of French from crossing his border."

Dirk agreed the margrave had no desire and no ability. "If the French do cross, they will create an international incident."

"If they do," she said, frustrated now, "what good will it do for Karl to decry it as a crime?"

"I agree, princess." He was as defeated by the facts as she. It was time she knew how severely he too was limited in aiding the Bourbon Duke of Enghien. "Two of my colleagues have been arrested by Baden guards. One escaped, thank goodness. He is in England, at last. But the other, I fear, sits in the Citadel of Verdun."

She put down her glass, appalled. "Two of mine have disappeared as well."

"It was Karl of Baden who ordered mine arrested. I would say he authorized your friends' imprisonment, too."

"You think it possible that the margrave would allow an intrusion of French soldiers on his soil and say nothing?" She stared at him.

He downed his liquor in one swallow and shot to his feet. "I do indeed."

She closed her eyes a moment, but when she opened them, she squared her shoulders. "I have failed, Lord Fournier."

He saw the toll it took on her confidence to admit that. Once more, he went to sit beside her and committed the faux pax to grasp both her hands in his. She did not flinch. Nor did she wilt. The lady could appear a virago, but was at heart a woman of substance. Given their recent acquaintance and the fact their first encounter was not friendly, he would reassure her of his compassion. "You tried to persuade Enghien. As did I. Another of my colleagues, also."

"My older brother, too." She took back her hands.

"Prince Rainer visited Enghien?" That was news none of his runners had given him.

When she nodded, so did Dirk. Bold of Rainer, particularly since he among princes was alone to publicly rail against French intrusion in German affairs and proclaim he would never yield his own domain to Bonaparte. For that defiance, he was as much a target of Bonaparte as Enghien.

That led Dirk to his next concern. "I must ask, where is Rainer tonight?"

She blinked, and her expression drifted to one of despair. "I do not know. I was last home in October, and he had left weeks before. He left me a note of what he intended next."

Dirk saw she told the truth. He knew not where her brother had gone either. He should. For weeks, his runners had kept him abreast of conditions in Rittenburg and the two principalities surrounding it. The little territory hummed along, its commerce good, its people prosperous.

Rainer and his father had done excellent jobs steering the members of their own Bundestag. Trained in democratic processes by Rainer's father, those men were devoted to their countrymen's peace and prosperity. Moreover, they were lauded as upstanding and loyal to their young Prince Rainer. His friend had no reason to fear they would vote to ally themselves with Bonaparte.

But Rainer never was at home to nurture his subjects. Weeks ago, Dirk's men had lost sight of him. Dirk feared the prince had either disappeared into Prussia or had been taken by the French. True, in Berlin no one boasted of hosting the popular Prince Rainer. But Talleyrand did not proclaim Rainer a prisoner of French hospitality, either.

"What did Rainer write to you?" he asked.

"That he would continue his work with his allies against Bonaparte. That he would never stop."

"And where do you think your brother is now?"

She surged to her feet. Her posture was that of a woman trained from birth to show fortitude and to command all before her. Yet she clasped her hands so tightly that her knuckles went white. "My best guess? I'd say a French fortress city. Verdun. Or Koblenz, where so many German revolutionaries terrorize their new rulers, the French."

"You think he is still on the Continent?" He had to know all the challenges Rainer faced. If her brother was in Berlin or Paris or even hell, Dirk had to calculate what current chances of success any German state had against Bonaparte. "Rainer is not in London?"

"He would never go begging to King George."

Dirk agreed that Rainer had always been too proud to go to the British monarch. But circumstances changed.

"Especially," she went on, shaking her head, "because I have not been a proper lady toward George's cousin."

Dirk smiled. "Good for you."

She stilled at his agreement, her expression easing with his approval. "Rainer might be in Berlin," she speculated. "They offered him funds to increase our army."

"Did he take them?" Dirk knew the answer to that, but again, he could not display all his cards.

"I do not know. I have been in Ettenheim and Strasbourg. Even my best friends, the Rohans, who are now related by marriage to Enghien, have no news of Rainer."

Dirk shifted the subject. "I understood he had been trained by your father that you were not only his heir but his chief advisor. Why would he not tell you where he intended to go?"

She spread her hands. "He does not trust his communications. Never into England. Never to me there. He always feared they would be intercepted. Plus he knows there is this rivalry between the Home and Foreign Offices. They fight in their little offices while we here suffer and starve from their rules."

Dirk had seen the poverty suffered by many in Rhenish cities caused by the French rules to restrict shipping on the river. "The French have no idea how to administer other people. One day they will pay for that."

"I have worked to make that day soon. So have you, sir."

"I am no one of importance. I do my small job."

"Convincing princes and electors to place their trust in the Prussians or the British. You may call your work small, but you have been successful. Would that Rainer could join you and end his travels."

Dirk had tried to convince her brother to do just that.

"I know," she said with a sigh. "You failed with him. You are here and have been since the Amiens peace began. You have done good work, all this time, traveling up and down the Rhine, slipping into Strasbourg, up to Verdun and back again. Heaven knows where else you have been in your duties."

He cautioned himself to not be too complimented by her knowledge of his work. He stood once more, and at the bar, he picked up a small plate and began to serve himself some supper. He needed a moment to think.

"Have you tried the ham?" he asked her as he forked a paper-thin slice, then considered the four pretty cheeses before him.

"What?" Laughing, she came to stand beside him. Her warmth dissolved his attempt to remain logical. "No."

"I like a mix of hard and soft cheese. What do you prefer? The blue? Did you try it?"

"No!" She put a hand to his wrist.

She was so close, he absorbed the need in her eyes. She could touch him at will. He could get used to that—protocol be damned.

"Can you not listen to me?"

He nodded. "I do listen. But you are here for help. So now I say, I will be more attentive if you tell me things I do not know. You must trust me."

She took a few paces to and fro, then faced him, stalwart but frightened. "I cannot go home."

Now *that* was news. He returned to the settee. Then he sat back, his gaze fixed on hers, took a bite of the blue cheese, and tore off a piece of brown bread. Digesting all that along with the fear she suddenly showed him, he dusted his fingertips and pushed away his plate. "Why?"

As the eldest sister of the hereditary Prince of Rittenburg, she was her brother's heiress if anything happened to him. German laws in Rittenburg allowed women to inherit in order of their birth. If Rainer disappeared or died, she would inherit all responsibilities for her little principality. Tiny though the territory was, her subjects were literate, rich, and hardworking. They produced, second to the town of Heidelberg, the most bound books and pamphlets in all of Germany. The city of Rittenburg sat on the Main River, a major thoroughfare east and west through hundreds of ancient German cities and principalities. The Rittenburg burghers were prosperous, selling books and etchings and producing wood carvings of excellent quality for doors, frames, and interior designs. The farmers outside the city produced a healthy crop of wheat and barley each year. Beer was a favorite drink and export. Cheeses and sausages came next.

She spun to face Dirk. The desperation on her face told him her situation was dire. "I cannot go home. But I must. I have heard of all our friends you have ushered away from the touch of icy French fingers. I need your help."

He wiped his hands on his serviette. "You are here. We are now friends. Tell me first why you can't go home, princess."

"I was discovered by French agents in Strasbourg a few days ago. Despite all my ruses, someone discovered me or remembered me. I know not which. But I do know I was chased by two Frenchmen calling my real name."

Dirk remained stoic. That she had come here to him would lead French agents to him. He had worked so diligently to hide his duty to Britain. But there was nothing for it now. If she led the French here to him, he too was lost.

"You have come disguised as a man."

"Dressed so, yes." She swept a hand down to denote her breeches and boots.

No man ever looked so scintillating. He crossed one leg over the other to conceal his appraisal.

"I did weave and dodge," she said. "I split from two of my associates outside of Offenburg. They run south to Lake Constance."

Which means you and I traveled many of the same roads today to get to Karlsruhe tonight.

"Sir," she said, barely audible to him, "if the French take the Duke of Enghien, it is not long before they will come north looking for me."

True. "Worse, once they leave here, they will go north to Rittenburg." Dirk rose to his feet, his desire to keep her safe as strong as his desire to touch her, comfort her, and keep her. He knew the next thing she would say. "And they most definitely want your brother."

"To get him, they will capture my two sisters and my younger brother," she announced.

The horror of it loomed before him like an ogre. *Dear God. Yes.* He ran a hand through his hair. "They'll use them as ransom to demand both you and your brother surrender." *And if Rainer were put in a French* donjon *and lovely Liesel were locked away with some vicious turnkey...*

Memories of the story told last June by his friends the Earl of Appleby and his lovely companion, Vivienne Massé, flooded his mind. Viv's sister Diane had been captured and hauled off to a Paris prison during the Terror. She had died there. Dirk considered the extraordinary woman before him and knew he would never allow anyone to take her away to any dark cell.

"I fear the French have issued an arrest warrant for me. I know the deputy of that man Fouché. He knows me."

"Vaillancourt?" Dirk was appalled. Appleby and his lady had told him horrid tales of that man's depravity. Appleby had also told of the deputy's desire to trap Lord Ramsey's beloved lady into serving as his mistress. "How?"

Liesel nodded. "I was a kitchen maid in his household."

Dirk stared at her. "What?"

"I am good at disguise."

"If he knows who you are, evidently you are not that good!"

She flinched. "Yes. I admit that. I hate to, but I do. But don't you *see?*" she beseeched him, tears glistening on her golden lashes.

And his heart swelled to overflowing.

"I must save my innocent sisters and little brother. Vaillancourt will take them, use them, and demand Rainer surrender to him."

Dirk knew her by her deeds, her word, her reputation. He and she had clashed. But they knew of each other and each other's sentiments. He could not permit her to think he did not care.

So he committed the greatest offense against her august person: he took her in his arms. She came as easily as a river to the sea. She embraced him and clung. He felt each elegant arc of her finely sculpted body. Her heartbeat. Her gulp to force back her tears. She was lithe, pliant in his embrace, and so damn delicious to hold. But he was her hope. And if he was to be her savior, he had to seal himself off from the urges of his desire. They would be allies. They would be friends. That would be all.

He pulled back and saw she had choked back her tears. "You have done well to come to me. I returned home tonight knowing as much as you that the French will soon confront Enghien. I predict they will take him to France at the points of guns. All of that means you are right. We will leave, you and I. Tomorrow at the earliest, or as soon as I can organize my household here." He smiled, like a father, a brother, anyone other than a man who saw her as the woman he'd take if he were free and as noble as she. "You will go upstairs and bathe. You will acquire a few clothes from me, I suppose. Though on second thought, I doubt they will fit you." He laughed. "My valet will have answers. But we will leave tomorrow. We are, I think, married. *Herr und Frau Schmidt?* Shall we say, from…? I don't know. Basel. I will have Bartel dig out a set of forged passport papers. Yes," he assured her with a wryness he felt with a twist in his heart. "I keep a supply for any need. You and I will go, sailing north up the Rhine to the Main and over to Rittenburg."

"Thank you." She stood back, flexing her shoulders as if she shrugged off his inappropriate embrace.

She had to, didn't she? But comforting her was his sole mission tonight, wasn't it? A spark of desire told him he'd do it again and again.

She tipped up her chin, cool, aloof at once, as if she wore a crown. "My little brother and sisters are so dear. They do not deserve to live their lives in a French prison."

"And they will not." He stepped far away. "You and I will take them to London, and all of you will live happily until the day you can return, free of fear, to your rightful home."

Chapter Four

S HE FIDDLED WITH the folds of the yellow cotton gown as she appeared on the threshold of the breakfast room the next morning. Fournier stood to pull out her chair and ask her to sit near him at the circular table. "I see one of the maids has a few items that fit you."

She acknowledged that with a grin. She had on a shift, a petticoat, and no drawers or corset. She liked stays to control the sway of her breasts, but the maid had none that would fit her. Trousers she really loved, and she hated to give them up. Still, she would be grateful and pleasant. "Thank you, kind sir. I have not worn a gown in many days. It feels odd."

He fought—she saw him do it—not to smile like a rogue as her breasts hung full in the gown. "The color becomes you."

She tipped her head demurely, though she hoped she did not blush like a silly coquette. She was a princess, not a tart. So she sat primly beside him as he passed her a scandal sheet.

He covered her hand before she'd had a chance to read it. His touch, like those yesterday, inspired a tenderness in her she'd not known from many in the past few years. Whatever this man gave soothed her, and she valued it, indeed yearned for it, more each time he dared.

The look in his hazel eyes contrasted with the caress of his hand. The light in his gaze told of sorrow and trouble. "Bartel cannot get false papers for a lady until later today. You and I leave here tomorrow. That cannot be too soon. This," he said, fingering the sheet, "foretells no good."

The news was bad. It announced that a contingent of French soldiers had taken up residence in Offenburg, south of Karlsruhe. Liesel knew they intended to be a raiding party, destined to head further south to Ettenheim.

Fournier was focused on all he had to do to help her. "I continue to prepare today for us to leave. Eat, sleep, rest. Our journey will not be easy."

TWO HOURS LATER, he called everyone in the house and stables to the green salon. She went, too, wanting to be near him. His presence was a balm, giving her confidence and hope, two things she had not had from any man in years. More than that, the memory of being held in his arms yesterday sang through her like a new and startling melody. No man, except her father and brother, had ever embraced her with such tenderness.

She shook off the distraction. Dirk Fournier was to be her friend. Nothing more.

Liesel perched on the window seat as he addressed his full, assembled house staff. Her frazzled mind welcomed his careful preparations not only for her and him to leave, but for his servants' future. As she watched him with his servants, she saw they cared for him, and he for them.

He stood before them, friendly but fatherly, his affection for them apparent in his despair at his parting. Precise and thorough, he told them they were to keep the house open and make it appear that he was still in residence. If guards came from the palace of the Margrave of Baden or from any other source demanding to see him, they were to say he had left hours ago to visit a friend in Rastatt to the south. They were to say he planned to return in a week. After that, they were to remain, going about their normal duties for at least two more weeks before closing up the house permanently.

To each servant, he gave wages for another four months. He thanked them for their kind service over the past two years. His cousin Wilhelm Leber, who lived in Durlach, at the older, eastern edge of the city, would provide all with good references. Leber would say he had been their employer for the past two years. Therefore, none of them need fear retaliation by the French or their margrave, if either should be so rash as to attempt it.

Though Dirk wished he could say he would return to them before the four months ended, he could not promise that. He cited his grandmother, who'd loved this little town and spoken often to him of the grace of those who lived here. He expressed heartfelt wishes he might stay, but circumstances concerning the French and their own ruler, the margrave, meant that, as a British citizen, he had to leave.

They buzzed in alarm.

"I urge you to remain calm," he told them, his hands up as if he were cautioning children not to fear a dragon. "We have all heard the rumors this morning of the French crossing the Rhine into Baden. We have no confirmation of that from the palace this morning, but I am certain the margrave would issue an alarm were that a possibility. Rest assured that I doubt the French will come here to Karlsruhe. They have no reason for it. You are safe. If anyone comes, they will come for me only, and I will be away soon into the mist. Now, one more note. The lady who is my guest"—he smiled at Liesel and kept her nameless—"and who arrived here last night comes with me. For those of you who have learned her name, I ask you to be discreet and speak of her not at all outside the walls of this house. It is her life we save by doing so."

At Dirk's dismissal, they went away, many in anguish, a few in tears, all in dismay. More news from the south had come from a merchant of cheeses who had come to the kitchen door. He blurted that he'd heard a rumor that French gendarmes and five thousand soldiers had come to seize the Bourbon heir to the throne of France.

Fournier closed the salon doors after his servants had left him. "They are fine people. I fear for them."

"You are well liked. They will miss you. I understand why. You have thought of their welfare as well as your own. And mine, too." *How was he so generous?* She knew few men his equal. "I fear I am taking you away from your home and your duty before you are ready."

He poured them both coffee from the sideboard and strode toward her as she sat on the settee. He put the cups before her, then returned to bring two plates heaped with healthy slices of strudel. His smile was rueful. "Careful, Your Highness. You sound as if you may find me acceptable."

"I do," she confessed. She'd known so many men, titled, wealthy, self-seeking. "I have not been fair to you."

His gaze locked on hers, and in that moment, she felt a stir of interest that had no basis in their plight or their shared mission. She had never experienced such a pull of her desire, and she blinked at the force.

"You are not to blame for our need to leave Karlsruhe. Circumstances demand it. It is time for me to leave here, and it is high time for you to return home. Rainer works somewhere, God knows where that is, and your sisters and brother are now our right concern."

But within her, a great new fear rose. All for him. "Many know where you live and how you have escorted so many princes and dukes from their confiscated lands to safety. The French mark that against you. Someone will come to take you away. Someone will look for you."

He shook his head, then took a drink of his coffee. "Do not fear, princess. Put your mind to the task and push aside your fears. I have ordered diversions. You and I will go undetected."

He'd told her that yesterday he had ordered his houseman, Bartel, to pension two of the staff. Bartel was to send out a man and a woman who had the same height and weight as his lordship and her. On the Rhine, the former footman and upstairs maid were to hire a boat south to Basel, Switzerland. They were to take moderate accommodations, stay for a day or two to note if anyone followed them. Then, seeing themselves clear, they were to head toward Stuttgart, going by way of small towns. Eventually, within five or six days, if they were not followed, they could return to their families in Baden. His lordship had given them more than enough German coin to cover their expenses.

Fournier did the same with another set of his former staff that very day. Sending off a male house servant and a former lady's maid, Fournier ordered them to travel northwest toward Kaiserslautern. That route took them nearer French territory, a good deflection for a man who should not seek the company of any French.

It was not until the next morning that Bartel had secured papers for "Frau Schmidt" so that the two of them could leave. Soon after a hearty meal of sausage, eggs, brown bread, and coffee, they left his house at dawn. For expediency, they rode away from the little capital of Baden on horseback, he in simple burgher's attire he told her he'd kept in his wardrobe, she in men's attire that had belonged to Fournier's valet Otto. Prudently, they did not sail the Rhine. They could not predict if French forces commanded boats or barges up river. It was faster to go by water, but it was also more dangerous.

They both traveled quickly north, undisturbed as two riders of nimble, sturdy horses. Then, in a small village east of Karlsruhe, Fournier had bargained his two fine mounts for the purchase of an old Berliner.

Now, he and she made their way northeast to Heidelberg. He told her he had friends in the old university town. "One is a professor of chemistry. His wife is his assistant with experiments. They make a merry couple, a marriage built of mutual interests."

Fournier told her that Professor Neuhaus and his wife, Gertrude, would welcome him and his friend without any questions. "They know my purpose here."

That was so. In his friends' grand old sandstone gatehouse high on the banks of the Neckar River, his friends took one look at Fournier and welcomed him as if he were family. About Liesel, they asked not who she was, nor why she wore men's clothes. They simply accepted her. Diedrich Fournier was that well known to them.

But those in the ancient university town were nervous. French soldiers strolled the narrow streets. Armed and belligerent, they called out insults to many residents.

"If you talk back," his friend warned them that night at supper, "you can be arrested for breaking the peace."

Being sensible, the couple offered them the makeshift bedroom in their rafters. Their large room was clean and neat, but had only one bed made of numerous eiderdowns.

When Liesel saw the size of it, she put her hand to Fournier's to stop him from making an arrangement of pillows on the wooden floor. She'd expected these kinds of accommodations from the moment he had told he would help her get to Rittenburg.

"You will join me on that pile of feathers." She shook her head. "You need your rest as well as I. We can lie together and not *be* together."

He readily agreed. For that, she was grateful—even if, in the wee hours, their bodies moved toward each other, and at the merest touch of hand to arm, or fingers to waist, one of the two would waken, startle at the proximity, and move away. That was only natural, wasn't it, for people who were joined together only out of purpose?

They stayed for two nights with the Neuhauses, eating heartily, strolling their hosts' garden, and sleeping like the dead. The only reason they remained that long was that more French soldiers patrolled the streets the next day. Leaving through the massive Tor gates was not possible, as the French blocked the passage across the river.

The professor declared it unsafe to try to cross. "Your papers are good, Dirk, but we don't want to test *how* good, do we?"

But the third morning the two of them had been there, the streets were clear. The French had gone. South, said rumors.

Liesel was happy to leave late that morning to climb into a sumptuous traveling coach that Fournier had hired. Off they went northwest through the territory of Hesse toward Rittenburg.

⟫⟪

TWELVE HOURS LATER, after three coaching stops to change horses and dine, dusk colored the sky in skeins of blue. Liesel tried to sleep, shifting on the bench to get comfortable. Finally, on a huff, she pushed up.

Wrapping a woolen blanket around her, she sought to push it up under her head to make a better pillow.

"That is not working, is it?" Fournier's voice, rough with sleep, reverberated from his own seat across from her. In the shadows of the bouncing coach, she saw traces of his smile. "Here, take mine."

He was becoming more charming as the days and nights wore on—and it was his selflessness that she admired. What was more, he was one of a very few sincerely engaging men. Who else would pass the time in a miserable coach and make up poems with her? Or discuss the merits and demerits of Henry VIII's reformation of the church? "Thank you. But no."

He'd done so much for her. She would not take his coach blanket from him. The night was as cold for him…and she still felt guilty she had been so rash and attacked him that first night last year, when she'd found him in his bath.

She lay down, curled up like a cat. But for her long legs and arms, she'd fit. He certainly didn't. So much taller and broader—so muscular—he edged himself against the corner of the cab. She smiled. Last night their bodies' natural surrender to each other on their fluffy bed of eiderdown meant they slept through the hours and she awoke with his arm around her waist, her back to him.

"Not enough exercise today," he said to her with humor. "I feel the same. Once we get to your palace, we will have to avail ourselves of the gardens before we hurry off to England."

She pushed her straggling hair back from her face and closed her eyes. "We'll hike up the hills and practice our fencing."

"You fence?" he asked with a chuckle in his voice. In the darkened coach, she could not view him clearly. He was a silhouette against the moonlit sky, a big man with platinum hair expertly cut and combed but ruffled now, a handsome creature with long face and handsome, square jaw.

"Why not?" she teased. "Don't you?"

"A mark of a man's worth? Ha! I went to Heidelberg, Fräulein. Yes indeed, I do fence."

"Good. We can wear each other out."

"I have not practiced in a long time."

"Now, then. It will do you good."

He traced a finger from his temple to the arch of his cheek. "I once thought little of the sport."

She leaned forward. "A scar? I wondered. It's healed now. Do you mean to tell me that you won't take it up?"

"I do." He crossed his arms. "My cut was deep. I bled like a stuck pig. I care not to do it again. You understand, I'm sure."

"So we will play with covered tips. Just for fun. No need to mar each other's beauty."

He gave her a lopsided grin. "There is no time when I would try to do that. One's honor in university is never to disfigure women."

"I just want to play, Fournier." She snuggled into her blanket and smiled at him wistfully. "Don't you play?"

In the dark, she detected a distinct distaste for their topic. "I never play with women."

That took her breath. She felt singed. As the crux of his problem with British Society and the lady whom he was accused of ruining, did his vehemence tell her something else?

She didn't know whether he was warning her that he'd keep his distance from her—or if he meant never to be untrue to her.

PLAY? PLAY LENT a new concept to this task before them. Play meant fun. Play meant cooperation. Fencing was one thing. Walking gardens, quite another. They had no time for that.

He had no desire for it. That way was timeless ease, the wall between them opened with laughter and frivolity. He must not walk into that breach. For surely, that path led to more than the delight of awakening and finding his arm around her, his hips too near her own, his desire for her too evident.

He rolled up the oiled cloth that covered the window. The fresh night air cooled his heated head.

She was his charge. His duty. Never to be more.

"I cannot conceive of play," he said.

"No?" He couldn't tell if she were frustrated or simply curious. "Why not?"

"First of all, my princess, we do not have all the time in the world to play. We have three children to ready for a harrowing journey."

She threw him a scowl. Once more her look said he had not needed to be so angry. "Really, Dirk. I can call you that, can't I?"

For two who sleep together? Hell. Why not? Call me infatuated. Consumed. Flummoxed!

She sat forward and fixed him with the hard eye of a royal who knew her power. "We have servants. They will pack."

"Pack! Do not joke." Oh, he was being a bastard now.

"Yes. I'm sure Mara will want her dolls and Nikky his toy soldiers."

"Princess—"

"Heaven only knows what Katrin will take with her. Cook, perhaps for her apple tarts. Kat loves everything she eats."

"Princess!"

"And don't you think it about time you called me Liesel? I mean, we've been cooped up together for days. I will call you Dirk, so why not?"

"No."

"No?" She frowned at him, acting like a girl toying with him. "We are friends by now, aren't we? I do hope so."

He growled and sat forward, grabbing her hands. He was not her friend. Well, yes, he was. But he liked her too much to be so removed a creature as a friend. She was too precious to him to even think he might lose her to anyone. "Listen to me, princess."

"Liesel."

"Ugh! No toys. No dolls. We pack a change of clothes and sandwiches."

"Well, that's not going to last us. We need—"

He groaned and dropped her hands. *I need to stop touching you. Stop looking at your eyes. Wanting to bury my nose in your hair, your throat.* They were together night and day. Stuck in small carriages. Tangled in eiderdowns. Tied by need and duty. "We need speed. We need to be away. Fast. Do you understand?"

"If the children are occupied in the coach, then—"

He cocked an ear. Put up his hand. "Wait."

She had to be quiet.

He shook his head. Outside, did he hear the sound of horses' hooves upon the road? "Liesel! Listen!"

She sat up straighter. "What?"

"Please, be quiet." Two riders. Two horses followed them.

She stilled. "I hear them."

"Take this." He slid his knife from his boot, and would have pressed it into her hand before she brandished a wicked smile— and a tiny silver stiletto of her own. "Ah. You came prepared, princess."

"Liesel."

"Exactly. I am pleased."

"I am too." She threw off her blanket and put her booted feet to the floor. "Diedrich."

Chapter Five

"Dirk." He leaned forward, trying to see whoever chased them. "Nice knife." Their coachman gave a cry and a lash of his whip to the horses. "Do you shoot, as well?"

She balanced herself on the bench as the coach lurched forward. She cast him a stern look of reproach. Then snorted. "Very well. Have you a pistol?"

He dug one from beneath the cushions of his seat. It was a beauty, too. Long, silver plated, with an ivory handle.

"My, my. That is lovely." She pointed at him and smiled, but she was still put out. "But did you load it?"

"Of course I loaded it." His attention was still focused on whatever he might glimpse coming at them from behind. Even with his dodging, he had challenges to see them clearly.

She bent, opened her small saddlebag at her feet, and extracted her lady's pistol.

"Nice," he praised her.

"Loaded, too," she said with an arched brow and great satisfaction.

"You surprise me. Constantly. *Liesel.*"

"So good to meet your approval. *Diedrich.*"

"Dirk." He winked at her. "No more arguments."

Her attraction to him multiplied, but the moment was full of danger. No time for admiration or conflict between them. "We must best them."

"Those who fight together are friends."

Their coachman yelled, working hard to harry the horses.

"Those who flee together should be," she replied.

"Now is the time," he said, and nodded for her to brace herself.

Their speed increased. She swayed forward with the surge, almost falling into him.

"What say you?" she asked him in a shout as she tried to keep her voice up against the clatter of their old coach. God knew she had trouble balancing on the jiggling seat. "Can we outpace them?"

"Depends—their horses against the fittings of this coach."

She shook her head. "Ba! It's old, Dirk." She'd gotten a good look at the fittings in the stables where he purchased it. The wheels looked new, but the two of them had not experienced much comfort. "The frame could crack with too much pressure."

He indicated his gun and hers. "We'll fight so none of that matters."

She nodded, her eyes locked on his as one rider came abreast of their window.

Dirk gave her one last, reassuring look, then knocked his pistol against the frame of the window. "A little closer, you bastard."

She eased toward the window and copied his position, her pistol to her own frame.

But the first horseman's partner came right up behind him, brandishing a very long gun that made Liesel wince. It appeared to be a rifle, one used for hunting. Unless the man was a contortionist, his weapon was nigh unto useless.

Dirk fired at them.

In a haze of smoke and surprise, she took aim at moonlight glancing off the shiny, threadbare coat of one attacker.

"Got him!" Dirk yelled in triumph. Then he fired off another shot at his mate.

She inched around the window again, aimed at a hazy figure, and fired. But her pistol coughed. *Damn. A fine time to choke.* But she glanced at his friend's very ugly face and knew she had to do one thing.

She fingered her stiletto and gauged how far he was from her. She waited one tiny moment…and flung it at him.

The man yelped like a stuck pig. A hand to his cheek, he yanked like a clown at the long Tuscan blade sticking from his skin. His words were blue, his tone angry, his blood dark.

She fell back against the squabs, grinning, proud of herself. "Gone!"

Dirk sat, eyes wide, staring at her with pride. "His pronunciation lacked a certain…" He circled a hand in the air.

"Precision?" She gave a shaky laugh. "I do applaud anyone who takes time to make good conversation."

The two highwaymen had fallen by the wayside. And their coachman yelled to their team of horses to get them on their way.

"I plan," said Dirk with a wide grin and no small bit of awe, "on keeping you with me."

She preened, teasing him with a shrug of her shoulder. "For conversation?"

"For self-preservation!"

THE NEXT NIGHT, dusk had fallen as their coach raced through the walled medieval gates of the city of Rittenburg. The gilded town clock visible for miles down the gently flowing Main River stuck half nine as the coachman approached the red-and-white stone Renaissance palace that had once been Liesel's home.

She leaned nearer the open window, the night breeze refreshing her as much as the return to her city. She'd not seen her home since October. That had been a hurried midnight affair to check on rumors that her brother had appeared there.

In Berlin, it was said, he had attempted to assassinate the French envoy, Anton Marchand, then flee home. But Rainer had not been there that night. Nor had he planned to kill anyone. So said their Burgmann, Herr Becker. True, Rainer had left her an encrypted note, denying any rumors of his attempt to kill the Frenchman. But neither had she heard, after that night in October, where her brother had gone.

Tonight she returned home to do the work that Rainer should have done that night. Any night. But they were not people who did the expected, the ordinary. Wherever Rainer was, he had reason to be there and not here. She knew that. She trusted him for that. Now she was picking up his pieces.

She shook away Rainer's failure to keep their family from abduction, then let a sigh seep through her lips, the wind blowing about her hastily pinned hair. She breathed in her childish delight at the sight of her graceful ancestral abode. Her throat closed with all the emotions rising up to choke her. For years, she had pushed all tender emotions aside, just as she'd been told it was her duty to do. But suddenly, her lips trembled and she could not stop them.

Dirk pressed his handkerchief into her hands. "A true beauty, it is. I have always felt rejuvenated looking upon it."

Liesel dabbed at her eyes. These past few days she was becoming a woman who wept. At the moment, she could chalk it up to arriving home. But she suspected that her display was the revelation to him not only of her fear and gratitude, but also of a tingling new emotion that stirred her to desire the affections of Dirk Fournier. All those feelings were delicate as lace, the threads bound together much too strongly. She should cut them, destroy them. But each time he touched her or smiled or curled his arm around her in the still of the night, she was more prone to accept his kindnesses, more eager to receive all the tenderness he wished to grant her.

Now, he was proclaiming he loved her home just as she had. How could she not smile at him and seek all his memories to thrill her? "You have been here often?"

"Three, four times."

She was surprised at that. He was a friend of Rainer, and her older brother was a man of great camaraderie with friends too numerous to count. Still, she had not imagined Dirk within those regal walls. As tall as Rainer and her father, as stout-hearted, Dirk Fournier was a man of the world, loving and treasuring the beauty that man and God created.

"I cannot recall the number, only the refreshment of it," he went on, his gaze sweeping the night, the stars, and the nearing edifice of the palace many declared as the finest in Renaissance architecture. "When I was studying at Heidelberg, a cousin of yours invited us to come. We were four Englishmen who gladly accepted. Your father and mother's hospitality and Rainer's welcome always made it a happy holiday."

She grew wistful, suddenly as eager as a five-year-old to stop the carriage and run home like a child. She'd race, yelling, full of wild tales, arms out toward Mama and Papa, who grinned, ready to embrace her and whisper words of love.

Her tears cascaded down her cheeks. She did not stop them, letting them flow. She was delighted, saddened. Tonight, her parents were not there. Both had gone to their graves three years ago. By their decree, she had left them. Little had any of them known she was never to see them again. Her return now with this man who was her new friend, with Rainer somewhere in the wide world, meant she would be mother and father to her younger siblings.

She could not wait to see them. Her fingers clutched the door handle.

Dirk peeled them away, cradling them in his hands. "You don't want to fall out."

"No, no. But it has been ever so long." She sniffed, ashamed now to let him see her so undone. "Too long."

He viewed the edge of the copse along the river as they took the turn into the grand circle before the main entrance. He narrowed his gaze, at once wistful, a longing in his voice she caught as poignant. "I am glad we bring you home, Liesel."

She inched forward to hold the picture of her ancestors' palace in her mind and heart. "When I left, they told me I could not return. Not for years. I was so…heartbroken and…and…"

"Lonely? You can say it. Only I am here to hear it, Liesel. I know what it is to be alone in the world and to wish to see those we love." He focused on their entwined hands as his bass voice fell to miserable depths. "One should always be able to go home."

In a burst of compassion, surprising her, she did not think before she asked, "Can you not return home?"

He inhaled, bringing himself to awareness. "Too many in England wish to see me punished for my supposed sins."

"They have already done much to hurt you." She knew the story of his past, the honorable, disgraceful, talented, mischievous Diedrich Werner Maxim Fournier, eighteenth Baron Fournier of Fournier Park.

He was related through his father to the Norman conquerors of France, and through his mother he was a distant cousin to the German Margrave of Baden and to the House of Hanover. As the sitting baron to a title and estate many centuries old, he had also indulged in the prerogatives of his social status. He'd become a talented gambler, losing fortunes and promptly gaining them back. Never had he become known as a debaucher of women. Still the accusation that broke him was that he had ruined one young lady and refused to marry her or claim her son as his own. He'd fought a duel for his honor, nicked his opponent in the contest, and, as the winner, left the field.

The lady had retired to the wilds of Northumbria, had her baby, and lived, so it was said, in a tiny cottage by the sea. Her family had barred Dirk from White's, his club, cast him from his investors group, then asked that he be removed from Parliament. White's was easy—Dirk left town. The removal from the investors was trickier—Dirk removed his funds. From Parliament, the task was impossible. Still, he had left English shores—and become an agent for Scarlett Hawthorne and, in the past two years, a savior to many German princes.

Inhaling, he looked at Liesel with satisfaction that burned away her sadness for him. "Despite it all, I do work that satisfies me."

She assessed him. Handsome, forthright, courageous Dirk Fournier. "You choose the most dangerous work of all."

"The same as you, Elizabeth von Rittenburg."

"With you," she had to admit, "I will be more successful now than in the past."

"You do yourself a disservice by your disclaimer, my dear." His endearment rang through her like rich, dark wine. His gaze twinkled with an admiration she'd not seen in any other man's. He was strong and sweet. His grasp held more of her than her hand.

She breathed, her heart a deep staccato as he pushed a curl from her cheek and crooned, "There is no work as vital as saving friends and family from despots."

Oh, her sorrow swamped her when she had to kill the urge to reach across the divide and kiss his lips. Princesses did not invite intimacy.

Instead, she sat in her place and gave him a triumphant smile.

The coachman slowed their conveyance and stopped before the massive steps and portico. The red stone castle glimmered pink and glorious against the pale yellow and blues of coming night. Even in the fading sun of day, she could see how the steps had cracks, weeds had grown up in the forecourt, the street had not been paved in far too long, and, at the top of the steps, the wide double front doors were still black with age. The iron fittings shone silver, but that too was marred, as if intruders with mallets had banged upon the ancient portals.

Whatever had happened here was unknown to her. She'd make certain Rainer heard her anger over that. He'd tell her all from now on. She was his heir, and heirs were essential to the continuity of the state. Had they not learned that after the Bourbon king and queen were beheaded? Had no one learned that last week, when that upstart Bonaparte sent troops into another country to threaten the only male heir to the French throne?

"You are right," she said to the man who was now her confidant. She was suddenly afraid to go inside and learn how her family had changed since she left them. "We stay only as long as we must. Then we leave with the most precious things we possess."

My family…and each other.

Chapter Six

"STAND BACK, LIESEL. We don't know who will appear." One arm out, Dirk urged her behind him after his pounding of the huge knocker brought no one in answer. He banged harder.

Liesel looked back at their coachman and footman, whom Dirk had ordered to remain at the ready until he and she were admitted. Even if their services were not required after arrival, Dirk had promised them, at Liesel's suggestion, entry to the palace stables, plus food and shelter for the night. The coachman held her gaze with wide eyes and pulled at his cap in deference.

One of the huge black double doors groaned open. But only an inch.

Liesel saw in the dim candlelight within only a gray beard. Then a gnarly hand reached out. That hand held a pistol. *"Wie gehts?" Who goes there?*

She held her breath. The male voice was rough with age and held sharp alarm. She could not see inside the gloom of the foyer to identify the man.

Dirk removed his top hat and smiled benevolently. *"Baron Dietrich Fournier und Princessin Elizabeth von Rittenburg."*

"Was? Meine Princessin?" The old door fell wide, and there stood their burly family Burgmann whom her father had loved like a brother.

"Herr Becker! Guten abend!" Liesel threw open her arms. Such informality with servants was never done among her family. But tonight, she did not care. She was too overjoyed to see him, to see that he was here, that he lived, that he remained when Rainer had not. Her father and Hans Becker had grown up together here on this estate, and each knew the finest working details of the farm, vineyard, and the city. Becker was the constant in a world grown cold. He even looked like a bulwark against the world—he was tall, stout, and utterly bald, with cerulean-blue eyes that sparkled at her through his tears.

He put his back to the heavy door as he squeezed her in his arms, and the two of them held for long minutes.

"I cannot tell you enough," he went on as he held her from him to examine her, "how we have prayed for your life and your health. Now your return..." He shook his head. "Your brother and sisters will be giddy with delight."

Liesel swiped away her own tears. She was becoming, as they said in England, quite the watering pot. "And I, Herr Becker, am thrilled to see you."

"Come!" He stepped aside and beckoned to Dirk to enter as well. He reached to the side of the massive door and yanked the tapestry bellpull. "I welcome you both. Baron Fournier, I am happy to see you again. It has been too long."

Dirk took a step inside, removing his deerskin gloves and great coat to give them to Becker. He shook hands with the fellow who was the *Kastellan* of the palace and took a look around the gilded rose-and-white marbled foyer. "We meet again, and I am happy to see you well, Herr Becker."

"You accompanied our princess home, baron. These are difficult times, and I know His Highness is in your debt."

"It has been my honor to aid her. I will tell you that she has been helpful to me, Herr Becker."

Liesel marveled at that statement. Firing her pistol to chase away their highwaymen was one thing. But Dirk could not praise her for requiring him to escort her to the country where he was sought like a common criminal. She'd thank him later for his kind remarks. But for now, it was a pretty piece to say to their trusted houseman who did their family business, ordered their finances, and watched over her siblings in this ancient maze of a palace.

Dirk nodded toward the courtyard. "Our coachman and his footman are in dire need of rest. Might we allow them your stables, food, and shelter for themselves and the horses, Herr Becker?"

"*Javohl.* Of course! Ah, here is one of our footmen. Fritz, bow to our Princess Elizabeth and her guest. Fritz is new to us," Becker explained to them, then instructed the man to care for the two men and carriage in the courtyard. "I shall ring for another footman. We have, I am sorry to say, only two now, princess. But we manage. Now, you both must be hungry and in need of rest."

"We are," she affirmed. "We have traveled for many days from Karlsruhe."

"No!" Becker scowled, ripe alarm on his jowly face. "Were you chased away by the French?"

"No," she quickly told him.

"We hear they came across the border. Bad business," Becker said.

Beside her, Dirk did not stir. They had agreed they would say nothing to alarm the Rittenburg household.

Becker did not look relieved. "We have rumors here of their threatening the Bourbon prince. Crossing the Rhine should be punished. We wonder if the sniveling Margrave of Baden has the…" He cleared his throat. "Pardon me, princess. I mean no disrespect."

"Herr Becker, you must never apologize to me for anything. I do wonder myself about what the margrave has in mind. The baron and I have read in gossip sheets that he did nothing to prevent the attack, a mark against him by all nations."

"Ah, but we read here in news sheets that the tsar has sent objections to Bonaparte."

Dirk balked. "Good. Does he threaten war?"

"Not in so many words. But do you know the margrave is the tsar's father-in-law?"

Liesel gaped at Becker. She had not heard that. She'd been too long in Paris, away from the court intrigue and gossip.

"The tsar must show his support for the little margrave, eh?" Dirk said.

"Related," she said with a frown, "as they are."

"Still," Becker said as he spread wide his arms, "we are happy you are here, warm and safe."

"So then, Herr Becker," Liesel said, "forgive me. I long to see my family."

"Of course you do, princess." He handed over their garments to the silent footman. "Allow me to lead the way."

Up the wide, rose-veined marble stairs, Becker took her with Dirk following. She held the banister, dizzy all of a sudden from the grand scope of her former home. She'd not seen its like in two years, since she had run away from London and the fiancé who raped her before he married her.

They wound upward, round and round, past her ancestors' portraits in their ruffs and laces. The men were arrogant, blond, and broad shouldered, all too smartly dressed; the ladies, awash in rubies and pearls, were confident and majestic. They all stared down their long noses at her past the grand first-floor rooms, which were for balls, investitures, and dinner parties. Up to the second landing, they passed the portraits of her beautiful, golden-haired mother and her dashingly handsome father. She liked to think they looked down on her with some approval for arriving here whole, even as she came accompanied by a lowly but stalwart prince of the Bremenhavens and a baron of England. But then, did they even recognize her, dressed like a luckless carpenter's wife?

She had often imagined how furious they would be with Rainer for leaving their youngest children alone here. It was one thing to entrust servants, her father always warned, but in the dangerous atmosphere where tyrants grew emboldened to take what they wished, only the hand of the ruler should prevail.

Well, Rainer. You have abandoned your family duty here. Now I am in charge.

But, empowered by that idea, she felt a counter-surge of fear attack her—and her foot slipped on the marble.

Dirk caught her arm and her eye. "Allow me, please," he said as if he were her chivalrous knight.

"Thank you." She would not deny that she relished his assistance. She straightened her backbone and became the loving sister to those youngsters whom she had not seen in six years, and whom she now must save from the French bully at their door.

Dirk smiled, benevolent, his gaze reassuring her of his presence and her power. He had told her that he liked Becker and had met their Burgmann years ago when he visited with Rainer. Becker knew all who lived in this mansion and those who lived upon this estate. From the appearance of the outside, he had not been able to manicure the property up to its former standards. Liesel put that lack down to fewer staff and poor finances, not less devotion to his responsibilities.

As they took more of the stairs, Becker spoke with Dirk. "You would like your coachman and his man to remain in the stables, baron?"

"I think it wise to retain him for at least one night," Dirk said.

He and Liesel had discussed his concern for how they would take her siblings away from here. They would need a good coach. They would not, *could* not, take any conveyance in the stable block, as the opulence, if not the escutcheon on the doors, would announce to one and all who they were. That coach in the drive was no prize, but it would work for another night or two before it dissolved into sticks. Neither of them had any idea in what condition the animals or the conveniences in the stables were.

"If you don't mind, yes, Herr Becker. They both need to rest, and so do the horses," she said.

"After you see the children, Your Highness, you must want refreshment and rest." Becker's eyes appraised Liesel's shabby attire.

She arched her brows. "You can see we were in a hurry to get here. Indeed, yes, we need good food and a fine night's sleep. Tell me, Becker, do you have all my father's house staff, or…?"

"A few, *ja*. Here in the house we have four. Not including myself and the new chatelaine, who is responsible for the children."

"Where are they?" Liesel asked, her heart in her throat.

Becker knitted his brows. "They are finishing their suppers. Your oldest sister, Princess Mariele, heads the table. She has a visitor, a young man who is her beau."

Liesel set her teeth. Mara was only seventeen. She should not be entertaining a prospective groom in the palace alone at dinner. "And who is that, Herr Becker?"

"Prince Johann von Hartenburg."

The worst womanizer in all the German states. "Since when," she asked Becker in as steady a voice as she could muster, "has he courted my sister?"

"He has come every month for a few days since the new year, Your Highness. Lately, more frequently."

"I see." She cast a dark glance at Dirk.

He rolled his eyes, and they shone bright with purpose. "I met Prince Johann when we were students together in Heidelberg. An expert with a rapier and a stiletto—quick to solve a dispute with his skills, too. I last saw him when in November he came to visit me and went further south to visit with the Duke of Enghien."

So then—Hartenburg was a hothead. She would ask Dirk later if Johann wanted Enghien to leave Baden. But he clearly knew Hartenburg well enough to choose words that gave her pause. Not only did Hartenburg fiddle with Enghien, but he was breaching etiquette by courting her seventeen-year-old sister one year before she could be legally married. Worse, he was doing it here, without proper supervision of her elders. The man would give her trouble, but she would give it back.

She squeezed Dirk's hand to thank him for the knowledge.

He asked Becker, nonchalant as any visitor, "When Hartenburg began his courting, did he know Rainer was not about?"

"*Ja*, he did mention that, baron."

What did the English call a man like that? *An opportunist. A bounder.* Liesel caught a glimpse of Becker's profile, the outline of the dismay on his jowly face. She was furious and had to know the extent of the prince's intrusion. "He has not stayed or been improper, I do hope."

"No, princess. We have kept watch. Our chatelaine, Frau Ernst, always keeps company with the princess."

"Good. Even at meals, is Frau Ernst in attendance?" Dirk asked, holding Liesel's gaze.

"Indeed."

The chatelaine was new to Liesel, having been appointed during her absence. But she knew the rules of courtship, and this dalliance was not permitted for a young princess not yet debuted to the world.

She shook her head at Dirk in frustration. Becker still led the way and did not look back, so her voice was gay when she said, "I am glad, baron, you are here to meet my sisters and brother, and also to renew your acquaintance with Prince Johann."

He tightened his hold of her hand. "I would not miss the honor of making their acquaintance. When last I was here, I was not presented because, I do believe, all were still in the nursery."

The three walked down the hall, past the family salon and onward to the far corner of the main block.

From the far end of the hall, a dog began to bark.

Liesel's heart picked up a beat. She had last seen her dog in October, when she came briefly in the middle of the night.

At the family dining room doors, Becker paused with one hand upon the golden knobs. His brow creased with worry. "Princess, forgive me. I will be so bold as to say Baron Fournier's presence may be of help to us. Prince Johann is not known be cooperative. Even our chatelaine has disagreements with him."

"Is that so?" She gave a look of exasperation to Dirk.

He arched his brows, his hazel eyes twinkling in mischief.

An idea spiked through her. An older male added to the force she needed. She was not Frau Schmidt, but she could play the part if she had to. Her *husband*, she predicted, would go along with the ruse.

Behind her, Dirk inched as close as propriety allowed. His broad shoulder brushed hers. She welcomed the bulwark. Indeed, his strength was becoming not merely welcome but essential to her survival.

⇶⇷

DIRK WORRIED ABOUT Hartenburg, but at the moment, he wanted to know more about this dog that sniffed and scratched at the door. "If you don't open it soon, Becker, the door will be shredded."

Dirk felt a chuckle ripple through Liesel's body.

"Rolf," Becker explained.

Liesel glanced over her shoulder at Dirk, pleasure consuming her. "Best to brace yourself. Rolf is the real fellow in charge of this household."

Becker snorted and thrust open the door.

The dog was a small horse!

Dirk dissolved at the sight of the hairy wolfhound, half as tall as he, who sat like a soldier when Liesel turned up her palm to him.

"Rolf," she crooned to the animal as she petted his head, "I thank you for your welcome."

But the five people sitting at the long dining table stared up at Liesel, Becker, and Dirk—and they had a response opposite from the dog. Indeed, if Dirk were not so worried about the presence of that ne'er-do-well Hartenburg, Dirk would have laughed at their open-mouthed shock.

The chatelaine—whatever her name was—pushed back her heavy chair like a rabbit ready to scurry away. She was not certain who Liesel and he were, but this short, plain-featured woman had instincts that told her to rise and bow. "Welcome," she said with a crooked smile.

"Herr Becker!" The oldest girl who sat at the head of the table did not rise but took her time to squint at Liesel, then widen her eyes to appraise Dirk. Her examination took in Liesel's attire and his own, and since both were in need of a good wash, she regarded them with disdain. "Please introduce our guests."

Liesel strode into the room like a queen. "I am Elizabeth. Your sister, Mara. You recognize me. I see it in your eyes. Nikky and Katrin, of course"—her expression softened—"neither of you remembers me very well. But Mara, don't be a puss. Good evening to all you. Including you, Prince Johann!"

The man had stood as she spoke, a respectable look of greeting supplanting the surprise on his long, lean face.

"Liesel!" Katrin—a pudgy sprite of twelve or so—ran toward her, arms out.

The young boy Nikky held back, getting slowly to his feet as protocol demanded. All the while he stared at Liesel with wide sky-blue eyes, hesitant but blinking, clearly prodding his fragile memory of her.

Katrin hugged Liesel and would not let go. She beamed at her oldest sister. "I am so happy you are here. *How* are you here? Will you stay? How long? Oh, I hope you do not go. We need you! I need you! Oh, I am so happy!"

"Yes, my darling Katrin." Liesel stroked her flowing, golden-brown hair back over her thin shoulders. "I am here to stay."

Dirk batted not a lash at that. Liesel would tell them when they needed to hear the facts of the departure from their home. In the meantime, tonight, she had to establish her authority over them all. From the looks of it, Mara was reluctant to acknowledge the end of her own power. Meanwhile, Prince Hartenburg examined Liesel with curiosity tinged with resentment at the intrusion…and perhaps at the usurpation of his position and influence.

Liesel was undeterred. "Allow me to introduce all of you to my dear friend, Baron Diedrich Fournier. He has accompanied me from Karlsruhe, and we bring tidings of great delight."

Dirk assumed a formal stance and gave them a courtly bow.

Mara struggled to her feet, giving a forced smile as she went to embrace her oldest sister. A peck on Liesel's cheek was all it seemed she could spare. In beauty, she was a close second to her gorgeous elder sister. Her hair, wound up in braids around her head, was the same striking blonde streaked in gold, her eyes the same lovely amethyst. In grace, she certainly matched Liesel. But in graciousness, she sorely lacked aplomb and command. There was also an air of reserve about her, even resentment. She appeared older, flintier than her seventeen years.

But she sought to maintain her authority here as she stood aside, a hand out toward the dining table. "Please join us. We are nearly at the end of our meal, but I see that you must be weary from the road. Becker, did you not ask if our dear sister and her friend wish to retire first?"

That in itself was a usurpation of Liesel's prime place here. Mara wished to address Liesel and Dirk's cleanliness and attire? Dirk kept his smile to himself and waited as his savvy traveling companion put her sister in her place.

"Yes, Mara, we have just arrived. I demanded to see all three of you immediately. I am concerned about your welfare. Please, all of you, do take your seats. Herr Becker, Baron Fournier and I will have a glass of wine and partake of dinner. We will all have a chance to briefly refresh our fondness for each other."

Dirk could have applauded Liesel at her use of the royal "we."

Before she sat, Liesel went to her little brother Nikky and opened her arms to him. "I am so glad we have a chance to truly get to know each other."

He went to her embrace, but pulled away quickly. In his blue gaze was the question of a child who wondered whom to trust.

A footman quickly reshuffled chairs to make room for Liesel and Dirk. Another footman sought extra silverware and china and hurriedly put them to table.

Dirk went to Hartenburg and shook hands with him. They had met before, countless times, and it was only fitting he acknowledge their past. Then he went to sit beside Liesel.

All sat down. One footman serving at table advanced forward to push in Liesel's chair. Mara, much put out, pressed her lips together and threw a dark look of pique to her prince. The footman got to her before Hartenburg even rose from his chair.

"You did not tell us how long you stay," she said to Liesel.

"Tomorrow, my dear, we will discuss this," Liesel said as she appraised her like a mother hen. "Tonight, Baron Fournier and I are here to renew our acquaintance. All the news we reserve for later. Tell me, Prince Hartenburg, do you stay with us here?"

"I do, Your Highness, yes." The prince looked upon Mara with a smile that cautioned good manners.

Rolf came to lie down behind Liesel's chair.

"Have you visited for many days?" she asked Hartenburg as the footman came to pour her goblet full of wine.

"Six, princess."

"He came to keep me company, Liesel." Mara was now openly peevish in her reaction to her sister and Dirk's appearance.

"How good of you, Prince Hartenburg. However, tomorrow morning, I ask you to absent yourself from our family meeting. You understand, I am certain, my need to speak frankly with my brother and sisters."

"Of course, princess." He was downright unctuous. "I usually ride early. Perhaps, Baron Fournier, you will join me. We can renew our youthful acquaintance."

Beneath the table, Liesel nudged Dirk's ankle. He nudged back, then tipped his head in apology. "Perhaps tomorrow afternoon, Johann."

"Yes, afternoon would be best," Liesel added. "Baron Fournier will attend our family meeting at breakfast."

"Why?" A petulant Mara glared at Liesel. "He is not family."

"He will be."

"How?"

"He is my fiancé. We will be married soon."

Dirk covered his surprise with a broad smile as the others sat, gaping.

Liesel had established precisely who was in charge.

He would not refute her, by word or deed. By certain rules of conduct, as her betrothed, he would never have to display affection for her. But he'd already broken that rule and touched her. More than once. All of it improperly. All of it to give her comfort or support…even if his need sent flames to his desire to claim her with his mouth and his manhood.

But as his gaze swept those staring at him, he resolved to play the part of the swain. The man who'd marry her. The man who could love her. The man who could cherish her as she deserved. Regardless of her rank and his. Regardless of her reputation and his.

Yes, he grinned at her and raised a glass of wine with the others in homage of her announcement. He'd make her his wife. In a heartbeat. If life were fair. If he were another man.

If he dared.

![decorative flourish]

Chapter Seven

"I'M NOT GOING to bed right now, Hilda. I need to stretch my legs. It has been so long since I've been home, I must see it." Liesel regarded the young maid who had helped her with her clothes and a bath. "Go to bed. You must be tired."

The girl smiled in sympathy. "Allow me to get your mother's heavier robe for you." The girl had taken a night rail and summer stoll from Liesel's mother's chest. But parts of the palace could be cool, even in a warm spring. A robe was in order.

Minutes later, with candle in hand, Liesel strolled down the family wing of the third-floor suites. As she passed Katrin's room, she could not help opening the door and peeking in. Katrin was a younger princess and not assigned a sitting room, only a bedroom.

From the open door, Liesel could see her thirteen-year-old sister fast asleep in her mounds of pillows. Two of the palace cats, which Liesel would bet were really Katrin's, slept upon the eiderdown at Katrin's foot. One was a huge mouser, a tiger cat, who peered at Katrin with green-eyed snobbery. The other was a white-maned beauty that dismissed Liesel with a yawn.

Smiling, she closed the door and took the few steps to Nikky's room. Inside, a scraping at the door alerted Liesel to what creature stood behind this portal.

Grinning, she slowly opened the door and suddenly had an armful of furry dog who would have licked her to submission. "Stop, Rolf! Stop! I just had a bath," she whispered. "I don't need another!"

She took hold of his chain collar and urged him to his feet. Then she went to her knees to hug him. When she'd been twelve, Papa had given her Rolf as her own. As a puppy, he had been a fuzzy bundle with a sharp bark. She'd given him the name to signify the sound of his voice.

"Rolf, old man," she whispered as, now alone with him, she fought tears to see him not only alive but also very gray in his muzzle, "I am thrilled you are still with us. Protecting Nikky now, too."

He burrowed into her bosom.

She caught her breath. He had missed her. He had no idea how she had mourned his lack in her life. But her father had refused to send him with her to England.

"Rolf is too big to travel so far," Papa had told her. "He will be a nuisance to your retainers. No, he remains here."

Liesel swallowed hard on the memory of how she had felt so alone, so betrayed by her parents' sending her so far with no one who loved her and no one to love her in return. *Not even my dog.*

She sniffed and stood, craning her neck to spy Nikky, his little mouth open as he turned in his sleep and coughed. Her little brother looked safe in his massive bed. She frowned at the fact that she would soon take him from it. *Life or death, Nikky. This is an unfair choice.*

She bent to the dog and, with a hand up, commanded him to come with her. "You and I will take a walk. Show me the way if I forget, will you?"

Show me how to reclaim the joyous spirit of the fifteen-year-old girl who left her parents, her siblings, and all in her home to go so far away where no one loved her. No one.

They made the central landing, and she noticed that four wall sconces in the guest wing were ablaze. Hartenburg would have been assigned the first guest suite there, Dirk the next down. Perhaps servants were still attending one or both. She'd leave them to it.

Catching her mother's robe up around her knees, she scrambled down the stairs with Rolf trotting behind her.

At the next landing, she stood deciding where to go. She'd seen the far family dining room when she and Dirk had arrived.

The family's salon was another she did not need to see. She remembered so well the happy gatherings of all of them there. Papa with his books and his snifter of schnapps. Mama at the pianoforte. Rainer and her, each determined to beat the other at chess. The other three were so young. Katrin and Nikky pretending to be knights. Mara with her two favorite dolls.

No, she'd not do that room. Not yet. She padded toward the formal reception rooms. The long gallery was where her parents would greet diplomats, electors, and other royal families. She put two hands to the heavy gold handles and pushed the double doors wide.

The aged splendor of it took her breath away. The walls were hung in bright red silk; the chairs stood as gilded counterpoints to the framed portraits of more ancestors who looked down upon everyone. When she'd been a child, she had often come here alone to memorize the names of those she, in her childish imagination, thought might know her.

There was Elizabeth, the first princess of the House of Rittenburg. At fourteen, she had been betrothed to the newly minted Prince von Rittenburg. The year was 1254, and Elizabeth came only with retainers to meet the man she would marry. She brought with her ten horses and four prize hunting dogs—and rights from the Holy Roman Emperor to deliver imperial mail in German cities.

She had demanded equality in her marriage, control over her household, and equal ability to rule the realm. She had refused to marry her princely fiancé until she turned eighteen, saying that only then would she decide if he were worthy of her. But at that age, so said the family records, Elizabeth had fallen in love with her dashing lord—and nine months later, she had given birth to the first of six children.

Gazing at the portrait now, Liesel saw her own resemblance to Elizabeth, with her golden hair and eyes like royal purple fire. The first Elizabeth had exquisite features—fair skin, broad forehead, long fingers, and the piercing gaze of a woman who knew what she was about.

Like I once thought I did.

Liesel shook it off. "What do you think of her, Rolf?"

The dog groaned and settled down, his face to his paws on the thick blue carpet.

"Still don't like her, eh?"

He never had, but as always, he was a silent critic.

She turned around to the other woman who had once fascinated her. "Fredericka of Bavaria," Liesel whispered to the red-headed creature who in 1570 had brought to her betrothed and her new home a fortune in gold—and her lover. "You still stand here, a legend to all women who must have love in their lives. And a torment to all my ancestors who wonder if we are descendants of your favorite, William of Ansbach, or your husband."

Fredericka was so well known throughout the German states that when Liesel had arrived in England and the Hanover courtiers took a look at her, they sought to find any hint she might be unworthy of their cousin and merit rumors of her tainted blood.

"But it was I who found fault. I who named my intended unworthy," she said to the portrait. "And I paid a price for that. Did you pay any for your choices? We do not know, do we?"

The family records had a gap in the years during which Fredericka bore her husband eight children. When her eldest son took the crown of prince, he was in his fifties and his mother had died the year before. Old tales told rumors that the new prince had killed his mother and taken the crown, rejoicing she was gone.

"Let's go, Rolf." Liesel slapped her hand to her thigh. "Enough of these people and their legends."

The dog loped along beside her as she opened the adjoining room doors. The throne room walls were hung in watered white satin. The carpet was red. The huge throne and standing scepter were in gold so bright that even in the dim flames of her candle, they shone like the sun in her eyes.

"Rainer should be sitting there," she said, once more angry that her brother visited others, attempting to persuade them to stand for Vienna and fight Bonaparte's rising influence.

The dog groaned once more and sank to the floor to wait for her.

"No need to grumble, Rolf. We'll return to this room before I go." She'd need an infusion of the power and hegemony that had prevailed here before she shepherded her family away from their home.

She whirled away, the dog beside her as she shut the doors and skirted past the ancestors who had abided here…and had rarely been threatened with attack or assassination. She felt the frisson of those new threats as she fled toward the stairs, the back wing, and the cellars.

"Come on, Rolf. To the best place of all!"

He gave a yelp as he raced ahead of her down the back stairs, carpeted for the servants who carried trays and furniture and baubles.

Down one flight, they fled past the smells of the kitchens. Down one more, where the biggest, finest room in the palace exuded the true spirit of Rittenburg.

The roughly carved oaken door she pushed against was at least twenty feet tall and one foot thick. It was so heavy that a hinge on a spring aided any one person who wished to enter. The room held the lifeblood of Rittenburg.

On one side stood eight rows of wooden barrels stacked sideways on ancient slats. Each barrel had a tap and a spigot. These were the wines of Rittenburg's vineyards, aging to perfection in handmade oak caskets.

To her right stood the other product of her land in a famous keg of oak, thirty-five feet tall, majestic in its domination of the cellar. Full of beer, the barrel had been fashioned by the first Elizabeth and her husband, to provide enough beer to feed everyone in the principality for two weeks if they were under siege.

In the air was the aroma of hops and grapes. She paused, closing her eyes, inhaling the scents of the huge cellar that made her head swim. She leaned back against the open door...as Rolf yelped and took off.

Alarmed, she watched him run, then sagged as she saw him wagging his whole body to greet none other than Dirk Fournier. He walked toward her around the other side of the giant barrel. His presence wiped away sour thoughts, and cheer swept into her heart.

"You can't sleep either?" He sank his fingers into Rolf's scraggly mane as the two of them approached her. He was in shirt sleeves and breeches, a tight fit for him, but his own were most likely being cleaned, as were hers. Informal as he was, the lines of his strong throat and muscular shoulders set off a stirring in the pit of her stomach. The breeches must have been uncomfortable, but oh my, did they show outlines of his assets that left nothing to her imagination. Why did he have to be so appealing at any hour of the day or night?

She straightened her tangled thinking and smiled at him.

Another thought washed through her, that she was pleased he had found her here and not amid the portraits or the throne and scepter. Away from them, she was simply Liesel. "I needed to remember so much," she said. "And you?"

"Yes," he said with a fondness in his voice. "I had many happy times here with Rainer and my friends. It is a glorious palace, standing the test of time. Your parents welcomed all of us regardless of country or religion."

"They were agreeable people, well ahead of their time." *In some things.*

Her bitterness over being sent away filled her once more. She dashed it away and walked toward the giant beer barrel.

"What bothers you?" He kept up with her.

"Nothing."

"Something," he remarked. "Something that hurts. What?"

She shook back her hair and lifted her face to him. She inhaled him, all lime soap and sandalwood. All virile man. He had become her saving grace, so surely she could share her trust in him. Yet years of living in the cold atmosphere of the Georgian court had left her wary of such intimacy. If she allowed him too much, would she be vulnerable to him? She had to be cautious. She had always protected her wounded heart by rigid decorum and a bit of bravura. If she shed it, would she know who she was? "Are we revealing secrets of our past?"

"I will give you one for one." He arched a blond brow, looking boyish. As if what she revealed to him would not be a minor trespass on her integrity. "Why not?" he continued, more serious now. "We have been together for days. Soon, many weeks to come."

He made no mention of her announcement that they were now betrothed. Why not? Was he saving it...for what? His disavowal? God, she hoped not. She could not be shown to be weak to her family and Hartenburg.

She strolled toward the barrel, the symbol of what her family was and what they had espoused. Power, honor, trust. She must give this man his due. "Even if I did not value what you tried to do for Enghien, I know enough about you now to trust you in your work for me and mine."

"I am at your service because of friendship."

He did not say his friendship with *her*. But she smiled, nonetheless, and took the inference. "And when we return to London, many will learn what you have done for me and my family. They will change their minds about you."

He pursed his handsome lips. "You are an optimist, aren't

you?"

Despite the hollow in my heart from the way I was abandoned? "I must have hope to pin my future upon."

He reached over, caught a tendril of her hair, and pushed it behind her ear. "Dear Liesel. Would that I could say the same."

She caught his hand and held it to her cheek. It was beneath her to grab for another's tenderness. Still, it felt right to reassure him. "So many value you here along the Rhine. That news must travel."

"It may. But it is not enough to change what has been my reputation for more than five years."

His tone burned her. Her determination to save him grew greater. "The gossips hang on to a juicy story for too long."

He strode to the huge spigot pipe of the beer barrel. "And the lady whom I reputedly ruined was destined for a viscount. What I did do was unforgivable."

She stared at him. "*Did* you?"

He was innocent. He seemed so rational, so agreeable. He'd proven it from the moment she met him, as he stood in his skin only and she accosted him with insults and accusations. At every step of the way, he'd been a gentleman, a protector—and now, more than her friend. How could he be the animal who had brutally ravished a young lady in a garden and be unrepentant? Even fought a duel to uphold his name, win—and yet still deny he did the deed?

He riveted her with his gaze. "No." He picked up another ceramic stein and filled it. The sound of sparkling pilsner tinkling into the mug reverberated in the cool, cavernous hall. "Will you take it?" he asked, offering her the beer and his denial.

"Yes." She drank, filling herself with the fact that he told her the truth.

He poured another for himself. "I will not tell you all the sordid details."

"I do not need to hear any of them."

His bright gaze took her in with gratitude that flared into a wild triumph she'd not seen in his nature before that moment. He stepped toward her, so close she could tilt up her head and admire the sculpted beauty of his lips. "It was not I who ravished her."

She lowered her lashes in acknowledgment. The past days with him had told her that truth.

"What I did do was leave her and refuse to marry her. I did fight a duel. Her brother, you must know, was a bad shot. His head full of whisky, he missed me. I did not miss him. I left the country. He still threatens to take me on whenever we may meet again, and this time, he vows his shot will hit home."

She raised her stein to him and pressed it to his.

"*Liesel.*" He said her name like a prayer. "I would never hurt you or your family, whom I love as well as my own."

Did he love *her*? She considered what that would be like. His life was demanding, exciting…and dangerous. He was not a man to stay at home and live the life of the country gentleman with a wife who adored him.

"Drink up," he said with a hint of smile. "We must seek our beds to rest for the journey ahead."

She took a few sips of the good brew and left her stein on the counter for the maids to clear. She took a few steps, Rolf on her heels. But she turned when Dirk did not follow.

He stood in the shadows, the candlelight flickering over his platinum hair and dour expression. "Know this. Once I have seen all of you safely settled in London or wherever you prefer, I will return here. My work, you must realize, is never done."

He took her breath away. She forced herself to stand tall and take his declaration like a woman of consequence. He was a man cast out, but striving with all his being to save others. That left no room for the quietude she wished for herself. He would not have a wife, children, or serenity on his estate. She was not thinking clearly to imagine him a country gentleman, hailed by his neighbors, loved by his family, his offspring…his wife.

She would not be so foolish as to imagine him as anything

other than a man devoted to the art of chance and survival for himself and those endangered by the French tyrant who frightened them all.

Chapter Eight

LIESEL HURRIED DOWNSTAIRS to the family breakfast room the next morning. She'd slept late and feared no one would be still at the table. After her encounter with Dirk last night, she'd gone to bed, and though she walked the floor for an hour or more mulling his declarations, she was so exhausted that she eventually slept soundly. That alone was a novel achievement after so many months—or was it years?—of fractured nights.

This morning, because her clothes were still with the kitchen maids to launder, she had once more sought her mother's trunks and her gowns, neatly shrouded in linen in the ancient, tall mahogany wardrobe. Though her mother's half corset was small, Liesel wiggled into it, breathing deeply and disliking the way the sticks pushed her breasts into serious globes. A simple pink muslin was her choice, though its style was decades behind the fashion. It too hugged her like a vise, but she had no choice except to wear it. Liesel recalled her mother wearing it on hot summer days. She lifted out the dress, feeling a tingle as if the garment had waited especially for her and this moment. But she needed covering, not a gown that invited interest by Dirk Fournier. That was a failed ambition. She huffed and donned the thing anyway.

As she swooped through the foyer, she picked up the news

sheets on the hall stand. The Hamburg press held the latest from the north and from London. A short paper from Amsterdam spoke of storms on the Channel. But another paper out of Heidelberg claimed that the Duke of Enghien had been boldly awakened in the middle of the night, then arrested by French soldiers and gendarmes. Carted off across the Rhine to Strasbourg, he had been caged like a common criminal. Taken across France at a grueling pace, he had arrived in Paris within days of his capture. There, in the medieval fortress of Vincennes in the middle of the night, he had been shoved into a ditch and shot.

Stunned, Liesel put a hand to the wall to steady herself. This was assassination. Pure and simple. Outrageous and illegal. It boded ill for all in power in German states who opposed Bonaparte. That meant they would definitely search for Rainer. Now, too, they targeted all her family. Everyone. She put her forehead to the wall, breathing through her lips.

Her head came up. Dirk and she and the children would have to flee as soon as possible. She turned, her back to the wall, and forced herself to walk forward.

She hurried down the hall and heard laughter from the cozy breakfast room. Her heart in her throat, she paused to admire Dirk with her two young siblings, all giggling. *Dirk could laugh this morning?* Did he know? Had he read those papers too?

By the looks of the table, Mara had appeared, eaten, and left. Liesel was not happy that the girl had disappeared before she came down. She wished to state this business of their departure as soon as possible, especially now, with this disastrous turn of events in Paris. Plus she feared the presence of Prince Hartenburg put that in jeopardy.

Dirk got to his feet. "Good morning, princess," he offered politely. No shadow to his dire warnings last night clouded his handsome features.

Her little brother and sister rose, too. Both seemed happy as larks.

She'd put an end to all this formality as soon as she had won them over to the need to leave home. She forced herself to smile as Dirk's gaze drifted to her hands that clutched the newspaper. "I'm pleased to see all of you still here. I apologize for my lateness."

"We understand," said Katrin, her eyes sparkling with excitement. "Baron Fournier was telling us about your journey here. It must have been very exciting."

Children had simple pleasures, and Liesel wished she had not lost hers so dearly, nor so young. But she would not be a harbinger of doom, not when they faced a perilous journey. So she smiled and said, "It was fraught with many interesting challenges." *Not the least of which is taming my increasing appreciation for the man you find so charming this morning.*

"I like the story about the two highwaymen," Nikky said with the enthusiasm of a child for adventure.

Liesel shoved down her pique that Dirk would tell them that and make them fearful of any travel. "Quickly dispatched, they were." She waved a hand and walked to the chair that Dirk had pulled out for her.

"I should like to shoot such villains," Katrin said.

"No, no!" Nikky responded. "Girls don't shoot."

Liesel's gaze locked on Dirk's. What had he told them?

"Of course they do, Nikky," Dirk replied. "I told you, your sister Liesel is a very good shot."

The ten-year-old pouted. "But that was a story. Not real."

"A real story, Nikky," Dirk said. "Your sister is the star of a real story."

Liesel thought better of this topic. "If you are both finished, I think it's time you went off to your studies. Baron Fournier and I will be up in the nursery to talk to you later."

Her plans to talk to them all together were destroyed. She'd try another tack. Meanwhile, a footman appeared to fill her coffee cup and present a pitcher of cream.

Nikky hesitated to go and grumbled, "After reading, we are all going to play ball. You said so, sir."

"I did," Dirk replied. "We will all go down to play after you finish your morning studies."

Petulant, Katrin and Nikky departed under the watchful eyes of Dirk.

Liesel caught the eye of the footman whose assignment was to serve breakfast. "I can serve myself from the sideboard. You may return to the kitchen."

He bowed himself away through the swinging door.

"I know what you are thinking," Dirk said when the door stopped swaying. "I did tell the children about our trip."

So then, he would avoid discussion of last night. *Very well, so will I.*

He went on, a hand out. "I thought it useful to disabuse Nikky of his perception that females are useless."

She tipped her head. "He is a child. Katrin too. I don't want to frighten them."

His hazel eyes darkened in shades of green and brown. He grew stern. "I'm all grown up, Liesel. And I'm frightened."

"Yes, as am I." She chilled at his statement and put the flimsy news sheets to the table. "You read these?"

"I did."

"This creates a greater urgency for us to go. If the French come here looking for Rainer—"

"We are a good distance from the Rhine."

"They can come as quickly as we have. We cannot spend another night here."

"I agree."

She glanced at the open door to the hall and made to rise.

"I'll close it." He made quick work of it and returned to pull his chair closer to hers. He began in a low voice that yesterday would have soothed her senses. Now, he made her want what would not be. "Liesel, we can go this evening. I talked with Herr Becker late into the night. He will send home the coachman who brought us here, and his footman. I have given Becker a goodly sum to pay them both well. I seek their secrecy about our looks more than anything."

"Wise. Thank you. If you think they should receive greater compensation, Becker can take it from the treasury."

"I believe mine was adequate. But I will ask Becker his opinion."

"Good. Have you told him about the two who attacked us on the road?"

"Yes. He says the roads have been filled with highwaymen of late. He has soldiers on patrol. But fear of the French is great these days, and their tax on shipping on the Rhine has made many poor as mice."

"So you think those who attacked us were not seeking the Princess of Rittenburg and Baron Fournier?"

"I am more assured they had no idea. Still, to aid us in our departure, Herr Becker suggests he come with us."

Liesel's first thought was that Becker would serve as a buffer between Dirk and her. She welcomed that, given Dirk's declaration last night. She must not grow fonder of him, but tear herself from any illusion that he could love or want her. "But that presents a problem. He must return here, and soon. Rainer counts on him to provide order and structure."

"Even for a few days with us, Becker would be useful."

She bent near Dirk to talk—and looked at her plate, hoping she hid her interest in him. This morning, he was dressed in one of Rainer's navy wool riding habits and a blue satin waistcoat. Worse, he still smelled of lime soap and sandalwood, an intoxicating blend that only added to her fascination. She would stick to the topic of conversation and ignore his eyes and voice and all those charming assets of his person.

"Very well. Becker comes with us for a day or two." Then she fisted her hands on the table. "I am concerned about Prince Hartenburg."

Dirk covered one hand in his and urged her fingers open. "He can be deterred."

Liesel sat back and slid her hand away. She no longer needed his touch. "Do you think so? He looks fierce."

He stared at her, her refusal of his comfort in his sad expression. Still, he came to the topic. "It is a façade."

"He is here to court her. Without Rainer and me here, she is in charge. I know Rainer would not decree it so, but it is the right of inheritance in this family. If Hartenburg gets her to marry him, she would lose hers to him. He would have rights here to rule as the male."

Dirk shook his head. "But now you are home, and clearly he is not happy."

"He must stay that way. No Rittenburg princess can marry before she is eighteen. Mara is too young, and Rainer would never give his consent for a change. He did not approve of my father sending me off so young to England. Rainer told me years ago he believed a woman should see the world and have her choice of men. I agree with him."

She had outraged the entire British court, as well as infuriating her father, when she refused to marry the man betrothed to her. She had believed there was a better match for her, a man who loved her. Had she been wrong to think that?

She reached out to play with a fork.

Dirk frowned, his displeasure with the topic apparent. "Johann is thirty-five. He has had extensive experience with the women in the royal families of Europe."

"That seals it." Liesel dropped the fork. "Our Mara is not yet a woman. She cannot deal with him."

"I am certain Johann would covet the prestige of your family name."

She pulled back. "He wants more than that, I'd say. He wants a piece of the family fortune. The heir or heiress to Rittenburg has wealth to match the emperor in Vienna. To the prime heir or heiress goes the land. The vineyards. The postal service we have operated for the Holy Roman Emperor since the twelfth century. Our bank accounts are unequaled south of Hamburg. Our personal bankers report to us first, then to the princes and electors of other realms. But even to each lesser princess or prince, the fortune to be had exceeds twenty thousand British pounds a year."

"*Dear God.*" Dirk blew out a harsh breath. "What a prize. I had no idea."

"Few do."

"Meanwhile, the Hartenburgs have fallen on difficult times."

She sniffed. "I am not surprised. Papa did not like Johann's father. He said he cheated at everything. His marriage, his tithing, his taxes, and, worst of all, the grapes in his wine. I must stop Hartenburg and take Mara with us."

"I know you will."

"Perhaps you might go talk with Becker to make more plans."

"I can remain with you while you dine."

"You needn't." She had to send him away. He was too kind, too sweet, too devoted to her, and she needed him far away. "Go. I am fine."

A flash of concern in his gaze came and went, but she saw that her dismissal surprised him.

"Last night, Liesel—"

She picked up her cup. "We need not belabor a point, sir."

He smarted as if she had slapped him. "I am 'sir' now, am I?"

"You always were," she said with such a chill that she swore she saw him freeze.

"I did not mean to hurt your feelings. I simply had to state what I intend after our arrival in London. You deserve to know."

Deserve to know? Do I? No, that's unnecessary. "I understand."

She had stood for so many years on her own. Alone and determined, she had found a way to leave England, take her income, end her betrothal, defy them all, and do useful work in Paris. What she had learned working in the deputy chief of police's household had aided the British in Paris. She would not be stymied here, in her own home. Not by Hartenburg. Not by tender emotions so new, so raw. She was grateful that this dashing man had helped her, but she would not lose her dignity to him. She stared at him as a small voice in her ear whispered, *Nor will you lose your heart.*

"You told them we are betrothed," Dirk said.

She lifted her head high. "A play for power. Well you know it."

"*Liesel.* I *want* to be your fiancé."

Was that remorse she heard? If she moved one iota, all her fine defenses against him would crumble.

"Even as a ruse, I want that. But I would be a scoundrel to allow you to think that we might have any future together beyond our arrival in England."

"I do not wish any future with a man." *Few would have me. Fewer still do I desire.*

His eyes narrowed dangerously upon her as he surveyed her like one who knew she lied. "My darling, if I had a future with a woman, she would be you."

"Go." She could not look at him. "Please."

LIESEL HASTENED TOWARD Mara's room, the memory of Dirk's desire singing through her like a romantic melody. He was more than kind or dashing. He was a damned temptation to abandon every rule, take what days and nights she might enjoy with him now and plan no regrets afterward. But how could she do that and steer her younger siblings toward their proper future?

She couldn't. She might never have a partner she cherished, but she would never shame her family by doing anything more damaging than what she had already done to keep herself free of a poor Hanoverian marriage and a French tyrant in her land.

She knocked on Mara's sitting room door. She had to talk to her sister and win her over. Liesel had little idea of how deep the girl's affection for Hartenburg might go, but she had to learn and persuade her sister to break with him.

Without any answer to her knock, Liesel rapped again. The young maid who had assisted her last night with her bath and clothes opened the door and bowed. "Princess."

"Is my sister here?" Liesel looked over the girl's shoulder, but did not see Mara in her sitting room.

The maid pressed her lips together, looking sheepish.

"Where is she, Hilda?"

"She left a few minutes ago to find Prince Johann."

"*Danke.*" Liesel whirled away, headed for the premier set of suites assigned to guests.

Her knock upon the first door in the wing was far from polite. But she had to knock a second time to get someone to answer. She was just about to use her fist to pound on it when Hartenburg swung it wide.

"Princess." He gave a sharp bow, quickly shielding the shock and anger that appeared on his face. Over his bare chest and breeches, he wore a red quilted banyan that he loosely tied at the waist.

Liesel noted his lack of decorum to appear before her so informally. "Is my sister—"

"Yes, Liesel." Mara stepped onto the threshold of Hartenburg's bedroom. She wore a white muslin day gown, the bodice askew. "What do you want?"

"I must speak with you."

"Whatever it is, it can wait. I will join you in a few minutes."

"No, I cannot wait. I must speak with you now. Come with me."

Mara took two steps forward. The girl was fully dressed, thank heaven, but her shining blonde hair, done up in a loose coif, was very tousled. Whatever had been occurring here was risqué. "Whatever you wish to say can be said in front of Johann."

"Prince Hartenburg is not my family," Liesel said, using Mara's words of last night against her. "You are, and I must have an audience with you alone."

Mara lifted her nose. She was two or three inches shorter

than Liesel, but her governesses had trained her well to appear inflexible. "Say it here."

Hartenburg cleared his throat. "I will excuse myself."

Liesel graced him with a haughty stare of approval.

"No!" Mara shouted. "Johann, stay!"

Liesel fought her own outrage. "Mara, you rile me. We are family."

"So is Johann!"

Liesel moved not an eyelash.

"He *is*," Mara insisted.

He took a step toward her. "Mara, *bitte.*"

"You are! You are!" Tears filled her purple eyes as she beseeched him to stay, then glared at Liesel. "He is my betrothed."

"Neither Rainer nor I have approved. Nor would we. You are too young to marry."

Beneath her breath, Mara cursed.

"Do not dare say more." Liesel spun toward Hartenburg. "Leave us."

With an apology in his eyes for Mara, he headed for the door.

"Tell her, Johann! Tell her you want me to marry you!" Mara watched him go and groaned in frustration. To Liesel, she blurted, "You have no right to do this."

"I do. You know it. Rainer is not here. I am next in line."

"Rainer is never here! What does he care for us? Nothing. He chases skirts. Goes to all the best balls. Flits around Germany like a stallion at stud."

That was something Liesel had not heard about her brother. Was that just a cover for his political activities? She would investigate that later. "He is the leader of this territory and of this house."

"He does not show it."

"He does not have to show it to you, Mara."

"Well, I do not do as he bids, or you, either."

"You will. I am here, and—"

"And just who *are* you, eh? The older sister who was to become part of the British royal house but ran away." Mara took a step toward her. "You refused to marry the man intended for you. Everyone in the empire knows that. And what did you do? You stayed in London and attended parties. Did you come home to 'look after' your family? No! Where were you, eh? God knows where you have been and who you have been with! A man? Many men? Now this one! This so-called baron!"

Liesel had expected her family to question where she'd been, but had not anticipated such virulence. Nor could she tell them what she had *really* been doing among the British *ton*. Let alone what subterfuge she'd engaged in once in Paris, Strasbourg, and Ettenheim.

"Princess Mara?" a man's voice called from deep inside Johann's bedroom. "What is the problem? Princess, I beg your pardon. Do you need help?"

"No, Fritz. *Danke*. My sister and I are speaking."

Liesel had forgotten that these guest bedrooms had small adjacent rooms for valets and maids. No doors separated the master rooms from the servants. Fritz, who must be Hartenburg's valet, had overheard them.

"Come with me, Mara. We need privacy, and we will finish this in my rooms." Liesel made for the hall. Even her obstinate sister must see that this argument was not fit for servants' ears.

Chapter Nine

“WHAT IS IT you want?” Mara took two steps into Liesel's sitting room. She took up a regal pose, her hands folded before her, her posture stretched tall.

“Close the door, Mara.” Liesel breathed deeply, subduing her dismay at her sister's appearance. “Your hair is tousled.”

Mara lifted one nervous hand to the tendrils escaping her pinned hair. “Hilda is not skilled.”

“Your gown is wrinkled.”

Mara folded her arms.

Liesel would have answers. “Why is Prince Hartenburg here visiting for so long?”

“He courts me. I told you. He wants to marry me.”

“Do you want to marry him?”

“I do.”

“I see. Did he come here with a formal proposal of marriage?”

“What do you mean? Flowers and poetry? A ring?” She was being snide.

Liesel suppressed her dismay at her sister's naïveté. “A document outlining your official role in Hartenburg once you are his wife?”

“I would be his wife. His consort, too, when his father dies.”

“But you have seen no document signed by his father that

offers you that role?"

A bit of the iron in the girl's backbone melted.

I thought so. "There is no proposal of marriage. Therefore, you leave with me tonight along with—"

"What? *No!* Are you mad?"

"Angry at the need to leave my home, yes, I am, Mara. Crazed that I must go and take you, Katrin, and Nikky? Yes! Absolutely."

Mara braced her feet. "I will not go."

"You will. Pack one bag yourself. Discuss this with no servant. And above all, do not tell Hartenburg."

"I will! He will take me away!"

"Without marriage? Over my dead body."

Mara fisted her hands and strode forward. "You cannot do this!"

"Do you wish to die in a ditch in Paris?"

"What? *What?*"

"Our father and Rainer are known throughout Europe as opponents of Bonaparte. Last week, the French invaded Baden and abducted the heir to the Bourbon throne. Then they took him to Paris, forced him into a ditch, and shot him. If you wish to die the same way, you will of course remain here." Liesel picked up her skirts. "Otherwise, you come with me tonight."

Mara tracked her to the door. "You cannot do this. I—I belong with Johann. He will protect me. He loves me."

"Show me the proof."

"I don't have it. Not…not yet."

Liesel cringed. *Please let this not be as I feared.* "What do you mean? When will you have it? When will he give it, eh?"

"He loves me. He…he has kissed me and told me."

Rage burned through Liesel. The man had taken advantage of her sister. "In England, if a man kisses an unmarried woman, he declares he is as good as married to her."

"Yes," Mara cried, squaring her shoulders. "Yes! He has kissed me."

"What else?" Liesel could not let this be the end of the discussion. If Hartenburg had been intimate with her sister, then to take her to England presented them with the problem of his potential by-blow.

Mara flinched.

"What else have you done with him?"

"Kissed him. Often."

"On the lips?"

"Oh, oh!" Mara backed up, her throat red as berries in her dismay. "You ask too much."

"I must know much. Has he done more than kiss you on the mouth?"

"Yes! Yes!" Tears blossomed on her sister's cheeks.

Liesel wanted to scream. "Are you no longer a maiden?"

"I...I...don't know."

Liesel gulped. Her poor sister. This was the result of Mara lacking a mother and an older sister. This was not her fault, but if there were a child from this, then Johann von Hartenburg was the father. "Stay here."

"Where are you going?" Mara was right behind her, pulling on her sleeve.

"Let go, Mara." Liesel gave her the stare she had practiced on the likes of the English Queen Charlotte and her nobles. "Do not leave this room."

The girl swiped tears from her red face. "I belong to Johann! I won't leave with you tonight. You cannot make me."

"We shall see."

"GOOD MORNING, HERR Becker." Dirk had looked for the Rittenburg Burgmann in his office in the palace, but a footman had told him to find the man in the stables. "How are you? I hoped we might talk again privately."

Two grooms shod a horse. The others, including the coachman and footman Dirk had hired in the south, were out walking the other horses.

The Prince of Rittenburg's stables were reputed to be larger than the Holy Roman Emperor's. Because Rittenburg had delivered the mail throughout the empire for more than six centuries, their animals and their equipage were the most sturdy, efficient, and modern. The emphasis was on speed and strength. The mail, after all, must go through.

Smiling, Becker rose from a squat. "Of course, baron. How may I help you?"

Dirk indicated the open doors leading to the racing track and the outdoor paddocks. No one was about to overhear their discussion. "I must ask for your advice on a number of issues."

"Anything you need, I am your man."

Dirk nodded and led them down the path to the observation platform in front of the track. No one else was about. "Your princess and all the family must leave here soon. Tonight would be best."

"I concluded, baron, that you and Princess Elizabeth came quickly and would leave as quickly. The papers this morning confirm that urgency. What has happened to the Duke of Enghien must not happen to those here."

Dirk winced. "Prince Rainer and his father did not approve of Consul Bonaparte. Ever."

"No, the Frenchman has his eyes on other people's lands."

"Now that the French have crossed the border to abduct the Duke of Enghien and even to assassinate him, Princess Elizabeth and her brother and sisters are not safe here."

"If Napoleon comes this far, he is a fool."

Dirk nodded. He hoped that statement could have more substance than bravado. But he had seen firsthand the power of deception in diplomacy. "Nonetheless, the princess and I will take the children away tonight. After dark. You fix the time, the place. But for that, I need a carriage of great speed. Horses of great strength."

"Unmarked. Not one of ours."

"We must meet that carriage on the edge of the city. I care not where. I leave that to you. But there must be diversion. Horses, carriages. Two people appearing to escape. Four others. A mix to confuse."

"I will do it, sir."

"I'd be honored if you came with us."

"As I am honored you ask me."

Dirk snorted. "Don't be too honored, Becker. I need your skill with a pistol. I also need you to speak for me. After all my years in university and in Baden with family and work, I can be noticed as the Englishman trying to speak good German."

"I think you have a disease of the throat."

His laugh was rueful. "Have had it for years, yes. But I also have another challenge."

"Name it. I am your man."

"I detect Prince Johann's interest in Princess Mara may be a barrier to her departure with us tonight." Dirk examined Becker's darkening expression. "I see you agree. Very well. I leave that matter to Princess Elizabeth to resolve. It is not my place to intrude. But I do say that if we have a problem with the young princess tonight, I ask for your assistance."

"I have an herbal remedy that I can administer."

"No, no. Nothing like that. But Prince Johann may need incentive to leave and return home. Do you know of anything we might use?"

"His father has written twice this last week, urging him to go home."

"Why has he not gone?"

Becker shook his head. "I doubt Princess Mara has refused his suit. So I would say it is because he has not yet asked her to marry him."

"What do the servants say? Does he press her in unseemly ways?"

Becker's pudgy features melted. "Perhaps."

If Johann had been the cad, Dirk would be the first to make him marry the girl.

"We have no strong evidence, baron." Becker swallowed. "Not yet."

WHERE IS HE?

Liesel had sent Hilda in search of Hartenburg. She paced the throne room, alive with nerves at the audacity of the prince to come here, take advantage of Rainer's absence, and accost her sister. Liesel had experienced how men could fawn over a girl and abuse her senses. Worse, she'd been attacked and raped in an attempt to show Liesel her duty and her place. She'd had enough of men's aggression to last a thousand years.

Becker appeared on the threshold. "Princess, you sent Hilda to find Prince Hartenburg?"

"I did. I rang for you but had no response. Do you know where the prince is?"

"Forgive me, I was in the stables. I do know where he is. He rang for mc in your brother's study."

"Outrageous." *In his banyan, the man walks my palace as if he owns it? Gall, pure gall, the man has. He even goes so far as to trespass into my father's inner sanctum. Is he searching for state papers?* Liesel's ire raged. "Bring him to me here, please. I will see him immediately."

"At once." Becker clicked his heels and marched off.

She faced the grand gilded throne that her father had inherited from ancestors. The chair could hold her father, Rainer, and her, and often had, as Papa took Rainer and her there to educate them in governing. Prince Gerhard had considered his role to be ruler, guide, and judge. "For that kind of responsibility," he'd told them, "you must have foresight and compassion."

Responsible for the delivery of mail throughout the empire,

her family had prospered financially but not been greedy. The wealth they gained from their service was shared generously with their people. The family became renowned for that, and for their acceptance of a council of burghers who made laws. Those enacted encouraged the growth of guilds, like masonry, carpentry, and printing. Farmers and vintners met regularly to discuss climate, floods, diseases of animals, and proper pricing of goods. Many in Rittenburg celebrated the triumphs that made the territory a haven for others.

After news of the revolution in France, her father had encouraged the council of burghers to even more democratic ways. "It is the mark of the future. We will embrace it."

Even as he worked ten and twelve hours a day at his regency, her father valued his lineage. He encouraged Rainer and her in debates about principles of fair government.

"But never forget," he'd told them as he sat on his golden throne of red velvet cushions, his hand on his ten-foot-tall, ruby-studded scepter, "who you are. What you must give...and what you must receive."

With that, he would order Rainer to sit on the throne, grasp the golden scepter, and tell him one new law he would propose, or one old one he would amend. After Rainer, he would order Liesel to the throne to do the same.

Her father's dedication to democracy and to Rainer's and her education had contributed to her refusal to marry an idiot. No matter his royal connections.

Rittenburg was rich, the envy of many German princes and electors. Liesel had met many of them personally or knew of them by reputation. To marry into this princely family was an ambition of many Europeans. Her father had planned for that. He had shared it with her before she left for England seven years ago. Rainer had witnessed the discussion and, by Papa's decree, had, like her, agreed to the stipulations.

"Princess Elizabeth." Hartenburg stood at the open doors, his banyan loose, his bare chest an affront, appearing somehow…louche. "Forgive my informal appearance, but I understand you wish to see me immediately?"

"I do." She took two steps and sat upon her family's throne as her father often bade her.

She pressed her lips together to hide her pleasure when his gaze turned to stone. Her position was not lost on Hartenburg. He stepped toward her.

"Am I to conclude that I am at your service?" Indeed, facing her like a subject, he was exactly where she wanted him.

"You are to conclude that I demand the truth from you."

He folded his hands before him. He was neither penitent nor patient. "I see. What is it you wish to know, princess?"

"Have you seduced my sister?"

He flushed from his throat to his hairline. "I have kissed her."

"More, I would say," she snapped. "From what I saw this morning as she emerged from your bedroom, you have done more than kiss her."

He straightened his spine. He looked…caged.

Good. "Do you have marriage proposal contracts with you?"

"No."

"Why not?"

"Prince Rainer was not here. Neither were you. I saw no need to bring them!"

Her elbows wide upon the chair arms, she leaned forward and seethed at him. "You came to persuade a young girl."

"She is seventeen. Old enough for marriage."

"Not of the age at which any Rittenburg daughter traditionally marries. Everyone knows that."

He put a gem-encrusted red satin slipper upon the lower step to her dais and leaned toward her with a menacing sneer.

Crowd her, would he?

"She doesn't care about your family's rules."

Liesel glared at his audacity to correct her and to belittle Mara.

He removed his foot. Set his jaw. "Mara was alone. Everyone

knew that she needed a man."

"So you thought you would volunteer."

"I did. Why not?" he challenged her, and did not hide his conceitedness.

"Ah, but I know why. You and your father saw the opportunity to claim our position and our wealth. Mara is too young to marry, but she is also too young to have benefited from our father's teachings."

"And we know what Prince Gerhard's teachings did for you. Made you such a witch that you became a scandal!"

She wrapped the long fingers of one hand around the golden girth of the family scepter.

He stilled.

So did she. "You dare too much, Hartenburg."

"Not enough, I'd say. We in the empire are in danger from that bastard Bonaparte. We need to be united!"

If he had not been so bold with Mara's affections, Liesel might have found that statement agreeable. "So you thought you would swoop in and influence Mara to marry you."

He lifted the ugly, jutting chin that he had inherited from far too many of the inbred Hapsburgs. "If she signed my document of regency, she need not marry me."

"Not—? Outrageous. You told her that?"

"Not yet, no."

She reeled in fury. "You seduced her so that you would have her sign authority for this realm over to you and your father?"

"Only until Rainer's return."

"Or mine."

"Or yours," he said without remorse, "if you ever did."

How far had he gone to win Mara to his scheme? "She tells me you love her."

For one brief moment, a look passed over his wiry features, one of a schoolboy caught in a prank. He rolled a shoulder. "Mara is impressionable."

Liesel flexed her fingers around the scepter and swallowed

her urge to hit him with it. "Show me this paper from your father."

He narrowed his silver eyes, a snake wishing to strike. How familiar he seemed in aura to that other man who reminded her of a creature that slithered upon the earth. But Vaillancourt, the deputy chief of police in Paris, was not here. She had not vanquished him, but she would this man.

"Now!" she demanded.

He inhaled, fury in his very stance, and left the room.

She sank backward into the fullness of her throne, draped her fingers over the carved lions on the armrests, and took deep breaths. Her heart pounded, but her mind was clear.

"Liesel?" Dirk stood at the door. "What goes here? I saw Johann stalk away. He shook his head at me when I asked his problem. Can I be of help to you? Or should I retire?"

She beckoned him in. "I am glad you've come." His presence would be a bulwark against Hartenburg's aggression. Dirk saw through the man. Furthermore, she trusted him in this—and she had riled Hartenburg. *I cannot afford to lose this matter.* "Stay, please."

"Liesel, I will not interfere. You can tell me your woes and I will gladly be your ally."

Dirk as an ally. Yes, she would take that. "What I feared about Hartenburg's conduct toward Mara is not only true, but worse. He will return with a document of regency that he intends to have Mara sign."

Dirk sucked in air. "How daring. It is against imperial doctrine to meddle in another territory's affairs. Does he have approval from Vienna for this?"

"I don't know. I did not ask. I fear I have not read such wording. My father never taught us of such a thing. But I must read it. See where my options lie. Have you ever heard of such a document?"

"Yes. If it is as I think, then similar wording has been adopted by Vienna when they wish to absorb a territory into their own control."

"Read it for me. Advise me."

"I will." His expression transformed from shock to gratitude. "I am no authority on Vienna's rules, but I will comment on whatever I do read that impinges on your authority."

He stepped toward her, and in so doing, one foot upon a step, he took a knee before her on the lower dais. His pose struck her as one of fealty. A knight, her liege, her man. Oh, that he might be all of that…in some other country, some other age.

"Anything you wish of me, Your Highness, I am yours."

In that pose he did appear to be her subject kneeling before her when Hartenburg appeared at the door. Now in trousers and frock coat, the man held Mara by her elbow. "We shall have this out. Even Fournier is now here. How charming."

Dirk climbed another step upon the dais and stood at the side of Liesel's throne. "Remember your manners, Hartenburg."

"Bring me this paper of yours, sir." Liesel arched her brows as he took his time. But he did let go Mara's arm and placed his document in Liesel's hand.

Printed on a press, all in Germanic fonts that tested the eye and the mind, the document was a declaration that those who signed gave over their rights to rule. There was a space for the signatories to define the date of enforcement. Beneath that, the one who signed would write in certain powers of ruler of the state of Rittenburg to the Royal House of Hartenburg, Otto, crown prince, presiding, and at his demise, his son, Johann, prince, or their designated heir.

Liesel gave no hint to her audience of her fury but, with her eyes on Hartenburg, handed the vellum to Dirk. He took it, silently reading, then finishing, his only movement to lift his stern gaze to her and nod.

"Mara, you are right," she said. "Prince Hartenburg wishes to marry you."

The girl beamed. It was the first time in this room she'd done so. "I told you."

Hartenburg sent Liesel a look that could have killed her.

"Are you certain, Mara, you wish to live your life with this man?"

"I love him. He is…wonderful."

"Wonderful enough to make you regent here?"

"I," he spat, "never said that."

Liesel ignored him. "What precisely did he promise you?"

"I… Well…" Mara blushed.

Liesel tipped her head, innocent in her inquiry. "What? Please tell us."

"He said I would be his love."

"His love. Sweet. What else?"

"That I would have the run of his stables and that his father would like me. That Prince Otto liked pretty girls who…" She frowned, as if thinking better of this line of questioning.

"Who what, Mara?"

"Decorated a ballroom and danced beautifully."

"Prince Hartenburg promised you this for doing what?"

She reddened from her décolleté to her nose. "Being good. Agreeable."

"Agreeing to what?"

The girl pouted. "You're being mean again, Liesel."

"Did he promise you his title? His throne?"

"No."

"His name?"

"Not…exactly."

"What were you to give to become the favorite of him and his father?"

This she appeared to be more sure of. "Agree to go to Hartenburg."

"And to become his wife?"

"Well. No."

"What, then?"

"To let him…you know." Mara cast a look at Hartenburg for help, but the man was too busy boiling to care for her needs.

"No, Mara, I do *not* know."

Hartenburg cursed. "Stop this!"

"Tell me. What did this man promise?"

The girl gaped at her sister.

"Mara," Liesel went on, "I can summon a doctor to examine you."

"No!" Hartenburg insisted.

"Don't, Liesel! Please don't. The humiliation of it…"

"What did this man promise you, my dear?"

The girl stamped her foot. "To let him have me!"

"Did he?"

"Yes, of course! Why not? He is…handsome and a prince. Father would have loved him."

Liesel bit off the reply she'd give to that. Then she stood. "Tomorrow morning, you will marry Prince Hartenburg."

Mara's anxiety vanished in a second, and the girl clapped her hands together.

Her intended scowled at her.

Liesel continued, "I wish it could be done sooner, today even. But we must summon the Bishop of Rittenburg to perform the ceremony."

Hartenburg rushed toward her. "You cannot make me marry her."

Mara gasped. "Johann?"

Liesel gave him her most derisive smile. "My dungeon is old, Johann. Six centuries. But I can still man it. Shall I?"

"You would not dare."

"For the integrity of my house and my family, I dare all."

"Late for that, isn't it?"

She rolled a few fingers in the air. "Seize the day, I say."

"You cannot make me do this! My father will come for you."

"I doubt it. He will applaud your union. After all, marriage to Mara comes with her dowry. I know he needs it."

"Very well." He fumed, rolling his fingers into fists. "Your sister becomes my wife. Now I need that paper signed."

"Of course, tomorrow morning. After the ceremony, I will do that for you."

The man knitted his long, lean brows together. "Why do I detect a trick?"

"No trick, sir." She grinned at him, regal in her success. "When I give you so precious a gift as the right to take my sister to wife legally, I would not then maneuver to deceive you."

Hartenburg stomped from the room.

Mara, confused, narrowed her eyes at Liesel. "What have you done?"

"Encouraged the man you love to marry you…as he must."

"What's in that paper?"

"I will tell you tomorrow."

Mara rushed toward the throne and grabbed Liesel's wrist. "I demand to know."

"Demand all you like, my dear." Liesel lifted the vellum from her sister's reach. "You have your wish. The man is yours."

"I hate you," Mara spat.

As soon as she disappeared into the hall, Liesel put a hand to her throat. "I hope she finds the fortitude to withstand the audacity of Hartenburg and his father. I did the best I could."

"You had no other choice," Dirk declared.

"Most of all, I pray he honors her."

They stood.

"Mara has gumption," he said. "She may surprise us with her resilience."

"You and I may never know."

"I predict we will."

"Your optimism is showing."

He acknowledged that with a grin. "What's more, the cause of it is that I suspect you saw in that document the ability to save Rittenburg."

Heartened by his insight, she wrinkled her nose. "I did. I think we need to adjourn to luncheon and discuss all the right things we can do tomorrow."

He offered his arm in a flourish. "Your Highness, allow me to escort you into the dining room, where we will ask the footman for a bottle of Rittenburg white wine."

"And schnapps."

"I worry—how often do you drink, my dear?" Jovial, he pressed her hand to his bicep.

She took a huge breath and absorbed the strength of his character. She had found such grace in him. "To toast the good and temper the bad."

He chuckled with her as they took the hall and the stairs up to the small dining room, but his mirth was hollow as hers. Yes, he had acted as her chevalier, supportive, as if he were her consort.

But he would never be that. To marry her would be to tarnish her good name and her future. She would be marrying down to a barony, and an English one at that. Worse, she would acquire the disgrace of his own past. He would never make her bear such a burden. But for the next weeks, for their journey away from danger, he was, heart and soul, her man.

Yet he was tormented. As he prepared for them to leave the following night, he bedeviled himself over and over again with the sight, the scent, the essence of her and asked himself what heaven it would be to have this woman, soft with laughter and hot with love, in his bed and his heart. He had no rights to the lady who consumed his every thought, but for the next weeks of his journey home, he would fill himself with the delights of which one man and one lady had robbed him. And he wondered—listed, really—all the things he would have to do to clear his name, free his soul, and take the only woman he had ever loved and make her his own.

But the list is folly, isn't it?

His dreams did not come true. None of them. Ever.

Chapter Ten

The NEXT MORNING after breakfast, Liesel went to the set of rooms where Katrin and Nikky slept. She'd not spent much time with them, and she needed to prepare them for the arduous journey.

As Frau Ernst opened Nikky's door for her, Liesel grew alarmed at the sound of her little brother's cough.

"Nikky! Sweetheart!" She found him putting his toy soldiers into his valise. "I am so glad you will take these fellows with you."

"They were once Papa's and then Rainer's."

"A part of the family, then. We must see that they enjoy the trip to their new home."

Nikky gazed up at her with solemn sky-blue eyes. "A temporary home."

"Yes, only that. But necessary." Liesel swept her hand through the silky, dark brown hair over his brow. "Do you know the reasons why it is necessary, my dear?"

He coughed, one hand to his mouth, and reached for another handkerchief upon the nearest table. "Herr Becker has informed us every day of the politics. I know Bonaparte may come here."

She sucked in a breath. If Becker had told him of the abduction of Enghien, she hoped he had not included that the French

103

could come to take him and all of them away to a dungeon.

"Will he? Come here?" Nikky grew wide-eyed with worry. "Mara says he will."

Why, oh why had her sister done that? Liesel ground her teeth. Her heart ached that Mara would take such revenge as to scare their young brother with the threat of death by Bonaparte.

"Come here, sweet boy." She drew him into her arms. "We shall leave here so that we are far from that man's reach."

Nikky tried to look brave. "Baron Fournier comes with us, doesn't he?"

"He does. He is our friend, and he knows much of the way to England."

"I like him. I'm glad he will come."

Me too.

"Will he truly marry you?"

That was a surprise that had her bursting into a laugh. "Why do you ask?"

"The way he looks at you is…" He wrinkled his nose.

"Oh, that's… Um…"

"He likes you! I see it. Katrin, too." He pointed a finger at her. "And you are blushing!"

"Nikky von Rittenburg, you are entirely too old for your age!"

"Then we both are, Liesel." Katrin waltzed in from their adjoining boudoirs. "I see Baron Fournier look at you, and I know it is true love."

Liesel looked for words. "Really! Where did you two learn such things?"

Katrin giggled as she came to sit on Nikky's bed. "Mara and Johann. Where else?" The girl batted her golden-brown lashes like a preening coquette. "Now with the baron and you!"

"Ba!" Liesel stood and tried to appear matronly. "You two read too many fantasies."

Katrin gave a shrug of her shoulder. "But now that Baron Fournier is with us, we don't have to read. We need only observe!"

"I think," Liesel said as she prepared to leave her siblings to their laughter, "you two need to finish packing. I am leaving. Do pick out your best court attire for your sister's wedding. I will instruct Becker to come check the placement of your insignia on your coat, Nikky, and your gown, Katrin."

"Liesel?" Katrin was now serious. "Wait."

"Yes?"

The girl took a step toward Liesel, her green-blue eyes flat with concern. "Mara wants to marry Hartenburg."

Liesel nodded, but anticipated the question coming before Katrin asked it. "She does."

"But…"

"What?"

"How do we know he will be kind to her?"

What could she say to that?

Katrin swallowed, but tears appeared on her cheeks. "Mara has been good to Nikky and me. She was strong and brave. For fun, she'd take us riding in Papa's old moat. She read to us at night, and when we were afraid… Liesel?" She broke into a sob that she tried to stop with her hand to her mouth, but failed. "I want… I want our Mara to be happy."

Liesel rushed to her sister, knelt before her, and pressed the young girl to her heart. "We will tell her that today. How we love her. How we are grateful for how she has protected you and kept you loved and safe." She struggled to keep her own sorrow from her voice. "We know she understands how to give love and receive it."

Katrin scrubbed tears from her cheeks. "But does *he?*"

Oh, my dear little sister, where did you learn about reciprocity in love? "I believe he will learn much from our Mara about that. You did, didn't you?"

Katrin sniffed and stopped her tears.

Nikky still looked worried.

"Please. Now, get dressed. The bishop comes, and we want

to give him our finest regards. We will not say we are leaving. Nor where we go. Nor how. We are celebrating the marriage of our lovely sister to a prince of Germany. Our Mara will be a princess twice over, a leader among her people."

At eleven o'clock, they convened in the throne room for the ceremony. Liesel was shocked that her mother's white satin court gown fit her so well. The style was French, of course, but had fitted sleeves that fell over her wrist. She wore her mother's ruby and diamond earrings that Becker had taken from the cellar vaults for her to wear today. Her hair was up in an elaborate bouffant and caught at the nape. From the vault, Becker had also taken her mother's small ruby tiara. Liesel had worn rags for so long lately that all the finery was a shock to her when she regarded herself in the mirror.

The effect upon Dirk, however, was worth every moment of discomfort. His mouth fell open when she entered the throne room. "Words do you no justice, Your Highness," he said as he took her hand and, damn his soul, kissed her fingertips.

And as his lips lingered there, she had illusions of his kissing her on the mouth and her cheeks. The euphoria buoyed her for the challenge of witnessing her sister's marriage. "You look dashing yourself, sir."

He accepted her praise with a bow and a smile. "As do the others in your family."

Katrin was dressed in a white satin court gown with the sash of Rittenburg across her chest. Nikky wore the royal-blue suit that was a male Rittenburg's court attire. He too had a red satin chest sash, with the insignia of his rank as the second son of their father. Becker wore his formal suit of the same navy blue. Frau Ernst wore her best gown of blue, and her keys to the nursery on a chain around her waist.

The newest arrival was the bishop, an elderly man with kindly brown eyes. He greeted Liesel with a strong handshake and a paternal glint in his eyes.

"I am delighted to gaze upon you again, my princess. It has

been too many years since I was able to enjoy your beauty. Such a lovely woman you have become." He turned toward Dirk, to whom he had been introduced earlier, and beamed. "I gather from the way you look upon each other that a new announcement of betrothal comes soon."

For the second time today, Liesel noted that someone interpreted a great affection between Dirk and her. They were not wrong, but they would never be right.

"Indeed," Dirk said with a broad smile as he took her arm. "The wedding will be soon."

"But not here," declared the bishop with a somber gaze.

"No, Your Excellency," Dirk added. "You are correct. Not here."

The bishop stilled. "Wise. Very wise. Where are the bride and groom, eh? We must get on with this!"

Hartenburg appeared, pausing on the threshold to scan the expressions of those assembled. Dirk and Nikky greeted him with courteous smiles. Liesel gave him a nod of approval.

Katrin strode forward. "Prince, please do come to meet His Excellency. He has never met you. Isn't that odd?"

Hartenburg let out a breath and became the diplomat he'd been trained to be. "Not at all, Katrin. We travel often but have not yet met all the best people in the world. How do you do, Your Excellency?"

Within minutes of his arrival, Mara appeared. She wore their mother's white muslin wedding gown of two layers of Bengali fabric. But what made those present gasp was her veil. It was transparent muslin, twenty-eight feet long and embellished with the embroidery of roses and bluebells done by a women's guild in Dresden. The Dacca muslin was said to be as light as the vapors of dawn. The veil had belonged to their mother for her wedding. Indeed, she had wanted all her daughters to wear it for their weddings.

Liesel bit her lip. It would be so for Mara's wedding today. Liesel hoped she could make it so for Katrin's.

Hartenburg went to his bride's side and, with a loving smile, took her hand to lead her toward the bishop.

If that look upon his face pleased Mara, it thrilled Liesel. She had so many fears about this union. But she pushed them aside to embrace the joy of the moment.

"Come, princess and prince," the bishop bade them with a flex of his fingers. "We begin."

They were done in minutes.

A sigh went round the room.

Liesel had stood next to Dirk during the ceremony, and when it was finished, she reached out one finger to touch his hand. He grasped it as if it were a lifeline. When she stepped toward the newly wedded couple, Dirk was right behind her. His nearness bolstered her and somehow transformed the occasion into a very happy one.

"We have a wedding breakfast awaiting us in the formal dining room," she announced. "We invite you to join us, Your Excellency."

While the bishop accepted, Liesel felt Hartenburg's gaze drill into her.

He stepped toward her as her three siblings headed for the door with the cleric. "You have my document?"

"I do, Johann. After we dine, do come to my brother's study." She did not add that she knew he already knew the way. She was trying to be civil and create a good beginning for Mara's marriage.

Less than an hour later, Hartenburg stood over the parchment spread upon her brother's broad oak desk and growled at the additions to the text. "I should have known you would make it to your favor."

Once more, Dirk stood a step behind her. His warmth consoled her as Hartenburg's gaze chilled her very soul. "It is useful to you," she said.

"To have Becker in charge? Are you *mad?*"

"I conserve what is vital to our family and to our subject's interests. Becker is our Burgmann, our keeper of the castle, the domain, the vineyards, and our banking accounts. Certainly you did not expect me to hand over everything we are to you."

He narrowed his gaze upon her. "What can I do for you without access to your finances?"

"With Becker's approval, you have authority to command our soldiers. Fifteen hundred men, well trained, is no small force. Also, with Becker's help, you have access to our stores of rifles, cannon, gunpowder, siege supplies, and beer."

"I would be their commander?"

"You would be."

"Write that in there." He pointed to the place he wished amended.

She picked up the quill and printed it in the margin. "Anything else?"

"The dowry."

Ah, yes. "As of noon today, Herr Becker transferred to your family account with Rothschild this year's funds. He has instructions to do this each year upon the anniversary of your marriage to Mariele."

Something softened in his demeanor. Whether it was the knowledge of the dowry or of his military power, should he ever need it, Hartenburg regarded her with a look of kindness. "I do care for her."

"Show me."

"What?" He flinched, confused.

"Show me that you care for her."

"How?"

She put up a hand to him. "I will hear. I will know how you treat her. If it is with respect and kindness, I will be pleased. Becker will know of my pleasure…and then, so will you."

Though she did not specify what that appreciation entailed, his face contorted with the hope of those things with which she might reward him. "Good. I am pleased to be united with the family of Rittenburg."

Liesel hoped she might one day say the same of his family.

⟫⟫⟫⟩⟨⟨⟨⟨

DIRK STOOD WITH Liesel at the back garden gate of the palace to bid the newlyweds *auf wiedersehen*. Dusk had fallen and the night winds promised a cool, pleasant evening—a good night to climb into a coach and leave for a new home, far away.

"Will you join me for a light dinner before we gather the children?" Strain showed on her lovely face as he accepted, and they walked into the ground floor near the kitchens.

Up in the small family parlor, she walked to one window, kneaded her hands together, and returned to the window.

He went to the long sideboard and assembled a plate of cheeses and early cucumbers, then poured them each a goblet of white wine. "Come sit down and let the day drift away."

She spun to face him, a sudden smile on her lips. "Can you read my mind?"

He handed her the crystal when she sat on the settee. "I try."

"You do a good job of it," she said, and pressed her glass to his. "To the Prince and Princess of Hartenburg."

"They make a fine-looking couple," he said with satisfaction at the way Liesel responded to his attempt to lift her spirits.

"They do. My parents would be pleased at the match. They would be delighted if they could say he loved her."

"They might be able to, whereas we have not had that vantage point."

She tipped her head at him and grinned. "Are you always so positive about people and events?"

"My dear, you know I am not."

She took another sip, distracted. "I wish we could have given them the wedding festivities they deserved."

"A breakfast, a reception, and what else?"

"A grand ball. Mara loves to dance."

He put down his glass on the nearby table. "Do you?"

"Oh, yes." She got a gay look in her eyes that said such a thing was her finest entertainment.

He put out his hand to her. "Then let's."

She opened her mouth to object, but thought better of it all with one look at him. "Do you sing?" She was brimming with laughter.

"I do. I am good, too, my princess."

"Sing me a few bars."

He cleared his throat and began to hum a bit of Mozart.

"My, my. You are accomplished."

"Thank you, Your Highness. That is not all I can do."

"Oh?" She put her hand in his and stood, so near, too deliciously near. "Show me."

Though those were the words she had used on Hartenburg, for him, they were a risqué challenge. He wrapped one arm around her waist and lowered his head so that her breath was his. "This is no pose for dancing," he said so low he barely heard himself.

"We can pretend."

"No pretense necessary."

She lowered her gaze to his lips. "None."

But he did not move, could not. He lifted his head to blink away the ambition to taste her, all of her. When he came back to admiring her smiling face, he took one step back. "We shall do a country dance. English. Harvest time. Simple."

"Instruct me, sir."

"We are a group of four couples. You and I are couple number one."

"And we lead."

"We do." He put one hand behind his back, lest he haul her against him once more and press her luscious body to his. "We take three steps in to the center and bow. Our opposite couple does the same. We go back and go to our right, where we greet that couple the same way. Then the last couple."

"Yes! I have done this dance in London. So now, we promenade to our right and change partners with that couple."

"Exactly," he said as they followed the steps, and he grew lonely at not holding her hand any longer. "I want you back," he said when he took the part of the second man and swept her flush against him. Her satin gown was water under his fingertips. Her skin, he knew, would be too.

Her approval of his embrace shone in her dreamy smile. "Is there no dance where we don't have to share with others?"

He wrapped her close, her breasts warm against his chest, her long legs in the sinuous white satin aligned with his. He whispered, "Only one."

She wrapped her arms around his back and stood on tiptoe. "I want to do that one."

"It's dangerous."

"Most everything is," she said, her amethyst gaze wide upon him.

"The pleasure is short."

She brushed her lips on his. "How can you say if you've never tried?"

He sought logic and found none. "My desire to keep you forever could ruin us both."

"Where is your optimism?"

"Flown away, my darling."

"Oh, you are a sweet man. Then kiss me in the void. It may be all we need to bring it winging back."

Her words burned away all his resistance. He held her in his arms, all woman, all bright, formidable female, and here, she was his heaven. Her lips were soft and plush, her mouth open for his claiming. She sought more of him, and he braced himself to absorb her like sunshine and rain.

But he could not hold his balance, and so he broke away and bent to catch her up and stride with her to the settee. Against one corner, he sat and pulled her up over him. She sought to kiss his cheek, his nose, and his lips once more. Sprawled over him, she was a supple array of blonde hair, purple eyes, and long-legged nymph in white satin.

He tried to find some halt to his spiraling desire, but she was devoted to the art of kissing him. Fool that he was for her, he sank his fingers into her hair and held her while he laved her lower lip and plunged inside for the flavor of mint, wine, and intoxicating Liesel. He had to stop or he'd take her on this couch.

With her hair down, her pins gone awry, he smoothed the gossamer strands down her throat and across to her elegant shoulder.

She tucked her face into the hollow beneath his chin. "That was all too brief."

He would console her, even though he denied himself more. "I promised myself I would not do that."

She kissed his cheek. "I know."

"I would keep you for myself if I could."

"I would keep you for myself if I were worthy of you."

He glanced down at her, her head cradled in the crook of his arm, her eyes twinkling with the desire he was sure was the reflection of his own. He pushed hair from her cheeks. "You are too noble, too worthy, my darling."

"Not for you. Not for any man."

The pain in her darkened eyes set his guts to churning. "What are you saying?"

"I am not whole."

"I don't understand."

"You deserve a lady for your own who is intact."

He cupped her cheek. "Darling, what do you imply?"

She pushed up, away from him. Then she sat up.

The knowledge that some man had hurt her hit him like a stone. "Who would dare?" he asked.

"My betrothed."

He stared at her. Whatever the details, he had no right to ask them of her. She was, even with that simple admission, embarrassed to her bones.

She gulped. "He said it was payment for my refusal to marry him."

Dirk winced. "He raped you because you refused him?"

"I said I would tell the queen. The king, too, if I had the chance. But I never did." She smoothed the fall of her skirts, then stood. "So, there—I've told you how ordinary I am. You must not hold me in any esteem when I am a woman ruined. Taken by a—"

He stood and embraced her. "Liesel. Darling, what he did to you does not change my opinion of you. Nothing ever could. I know who you are."

"Tarnished."

He clamped her to him. "Look at me. Strong. Valiant. Capable. Devoted. Crown Princess Elizabeth of Rittenburg is everything a woman should be, can be." He loved her.

The realization ran through his veins like flame. He fought the urge to tell her. What good would it do? He could not have her. No matter what the Hanovers' cousin had done to her, he was still not worthy of her. She might wear this shame on the inside of her soul, put there by a privileged ass who knew no better, but she should not bear it. Would that he could replace it with the tender, loving care she deserved from a man who adored every little bit of her.

But with his own disgrace, he could do none of that. While she wore her sorrow over that man's treatment of her in secret, he wore his in public. Where others spoke of it, ridiculed it. Where he had few means to kill the lies. Where he could not set himself free. Never free so that he might claim her. Enjoy her. Lift her up as the stunning creature she was.

He set her from him, his hands to her shoulders. "He hurt you. He brutalized you. It is he who must be punished. He who must suffer. Not you. No longer you, my darling."

They'd come a long way from sampling the joy of a mere kiss. They now discussed a crime and its punishment. Her release and her dignity.

"We go to England, where I will find a way to uphold you,

and you will find a way to tell them all how he defiled you and destroyed your life there."

He suggested they part and nap before they left at midnight. He was her man, her champion. No one would hurt her. No one. Not even those who assumed they had *droit du seigneur*.

NIKKY COUGHED AS he leaned toward Katrin and moved a piece on the children's miniature chessboard. The children sat opposite each other as their hired carriage raced northwest through the verdant woodlands of countless German states.

Liesel's gaze drifted to Dirk's. His showed a flash of concern for the boy. Nikky sat next to Dirk facing her and Katrin. When her brother coughed again, Dirk casually brushed his hair back from his brow. Rain had begun night before last, when they had left Rittenburg Palace. Becker had hired an old, unmarked traveling carriage for them that had taken them to a small village near Frankfurt. This morning they had set off again in another conveyance. But the hours saw Nikky's cough become deeper, inspiring Liesel to ensure they stopped somewhere soon so that she could nurse him properly.

"What time is it?" she asked Dirk.

He dug out the gold watch hanging from his fob. "After two."

They'd been on the road since nine o'clock this morning, departing from the small guesthouse where they had spent five hours in a cramped, old inn with hay for beds. What was worse, she and Dirk had feared being discovered. Without Becker to accompany them on their journey, she and Dirk had been at the ready with their pistols, lest they encounter any more assailants.

It was one thing to fight with Dirk, another adult, but quite different to ward off attackers with two children to witness the melee.

Becker had prepared diversions for the children with chess

and cards, Katrin's favorite doll, and, of course, Nikky's toy soldiers. Thank heavens that the children considered the journey an adventure. Liesel needed them in good spirits. The distance they had to go was hard enough.

Very hard. She writhed on the short bench. The pleading look in her eyes had Dirk nodding.

"I know of an inn, a fine guesthouse outside Koblenz. The owner has accommodated me often. We can stop and sleep."

"If he knows you, we could be at risk."

"Do not fear this. My friend is loyal. Have you ever been to Koblenz?"

Liesel shook her head and smoothed the brow of Katrin, who grumbled to Nikky that the pieces on the board shifted with the sway of the wagon.

"The Germans hate the French occupation," Dirk continued. "They save their own. Herr Heinrich will guard us with his life. He has done so for me twice before."

Liesel's head lolled against the wall of the coach. Of a sudden, they had come across a smooth patch of road, and her aching bones rejoiced in the small pleasure. "You have had an eventful life. I hope you had joy as well as adventure."

"I did. A lot of it, too. My childhood in Kent was filled with days spent with my father. He was an excellent steward of his land, and he imbued me with a love of plants and animals. I am very much like my friend, Lord Appleby, whom you met the first night you came to me."

She rolled her eyes at him, happy he said no more about that fateful event. "How are you alike?"

"I like putting seed into the earth and watching it sprout. I studied chemistry at Heidelberg, as Appleby did, and we two were the most talkative students in class. Disruptive, especially because we wished to know about British soil compositions. We learned about German agriculture because we had to, but he and I were always on about the differences in British soil. So I am a product of that plus knowledge I gained from my years visiting my mother's family in Baden. My other good friend, Lord Ashley, went on to Amboise, and later joined Appleby and me in Baden. I went home to Kent often. My parents insisted on seeing me. When my younger brothers each died of ague, I was left the only heir. But by then, traveling was in my blood. I had the urge to roam. My poor parents had to put up with me."

She smiled at him in sympathy. "You love them?"

"There was much to love, much to revere. I went away as a child to please them. They wanted me cultured, speaking many languages and knowing those in power on the Continent. My education was their prime concern."

"Did you not pine for them?" she asked, realizing too late her words indicated her own heartache at having left her parents and the rest of her family.

"I hated leaving. I adored them both. My mother is still a charming hellion. She is a lady-in-waiting to the queen, but often speaks her mind."

"I think I have met her." Liesel grinned at that recollection.

"She is a darling," he said with obvious pride. "I wish I could be with her as she goes into her older age. I miss my father. A great man, he was. And I missed his illness and death. Leaving home for my education was a sweet sorrow. Years later, I left home because I was forced to go."

Just like I was.

"Like you were."

She cast off the sad remembrance and rallied. "I rebelled. It is not what a woman of substance does."

"It is what a woman of conviction does."

She inhaled, recalling the way her odious fiancé had slobbered over his dinner and smelled like a brewery. The way he looked at her as if she were his to strip and swive. "I hated the thought of marrying him."

"As you should have. I have not met him, but rumor serves him up as a lout. Your wit and your charm would be wasted on him, my dear."

My dear on Dirk Fournier's lips sounded as it had on her father's. "My dear, they will love you." Or on her mother's. "My dear, you are the best of us. Bright and beautiful." She knew Dirk spoke those words in front of Katrin and Nikky to remain friendly. She let her gaze flow into his as she yearned for him to call her his darling.

But that was not possible. Not here. Not now. He would not claim that right in front of her family or the world. Katrin and Nikky looked up at each of them, questioning the drift of adults' discussion but not really interested in its meaning.

Liesel filled the silence with fluff. "I can spend my days in service to those who value me. But not on those who disparage me or ridicule me. Or ignore me."

"You deserve the finest gentleman as your husband."

She sniffed and shook her head. "I ruined my chances of that long ago."

"I doubt that," he said with conviction. "Some good man will appear and want you badly, Liesel."

Because the children were listening to them, she repressed all she wished to say about his being that good man. Instead she said, "You are kind to think so."

"Kindness has nothing to do with it—and you know it," he declared, a torrid response that neither child understood, but one that resurrected her remembrance of his kisses.

She did know.

But what happiness could it bring her if the good man she wanted would never be hers?

Chapter Eleven

T HE OWNER OF the guesthouse on the east bank of the Rhine near Koblenz spread his hands wide. "Welcome to the White Stag, *madame.*"

Liesel greeted the proprietor, whom Dirk knew well. That measure of comfort was second to her surprise that the man spoke to them not in German, but French.

"It is diplomatic to use French here," Dirk told her when his friend left to get room keys from his wife. "Since they took possession of the left bank last year, most try to appear inconspicuous."

She shivered at the knowledge that French soldiers could be so close.

He saw her reaction and leaned near. "They rarely cross the Rhine, my dear."

But that meant little, didn't it? The French took everything they wanted. Rivers and boundaries meant nothing to them. Heirs to thrones even less.

"I trust you are right," she murmured. She had little choice but to hope they were safe. Their carriage had arrived near dusk. The rain had turned the roads from Frankfurt into a muddy mess. Their journey had been long, cold, and arduous.

Liesel stood with the others in the entryway of the large

coaching inn, the wind blowing through in chilling gusts. Waiting for the innkeeper to return, she pressed Katrin to her side and put a hand to her little brother's brow. Nikky was burning up.

"I hope your friend has a cozy room available for us." The man had said he had a full house.

"He will make room for the four of us. I must say"—Dirk leaned closer—"I know of no other innkeeper nearby whom I can trust as well."

Katrin flinched when she overheard him. "I'm hungry."

Liesel cuddled the girl closer. "We will have a hot supper very soon, *ma petite*."

Dirk frowned, but said to them all, "Not to worry. Herr Heinrich will settle us. And once we are in, I will go a few streets away to a fine apothecary shop."

"I need camphor for the room, lavender and mint for Nikky. But from Herr Heinrich, I need hot liquids for tea. Every hour." Her mother had always been frantic to cover Nikky's little chest with poultices and feed him hot tea and clear soups. Her little brother had always been prone to coughs and congestion, especially in summer and autumn.

Traveling had contributed to his condition. She had to alleviate his misery quickly before he burned up with fever. And if he got worse, they could not continue tomorrow toward the coast. But she liked the looks of the inn. It was large, built of sturdy stone, and kept in good repair. She hoped that inside, the innkeeper wife's would be helpful for Nikky's needs, all of their needs. Most of all, Liesel wished for a well-appointed eiderdown bed for Nikky, perhaps even a fireplace in their room.

"Stop worrying." Dirk put a hand to her cheek.

She took his gesture with his generosity of heart. For a man so notorious, he was that rare man who truly honored women. Kiss her he may have, but only at her instigation. Take privileges and molest her, he had not done.

She gulped back her urge to turn her face into his palm and bless him with a kiss. She marveled that each day, each hour with him, she grew more reliant on him, and more her normal self than she had ever been with any man.

What was more, he merited her gratitude. His ready agreement to leave Karlsruhe, she knew, was motivated in part by his own need to escape French tentacles. But he had done so quickly to aid her in getting to Rittenburg. His finesse pressing Hartenburg to marry Mara was invaluable. That man would have escaped his duty to her sister if Dirk had not shown his silent but pervasive presence. His help with the hiring of horses and coaches, his knowledge of inns and the rivers, was all so vital. Had he not agreed to help her, she alone could not have managed so well with two children in tow, one of whom was very ill.

Dirk took his hand away, but his smile remained. "We will be well. All of us."

Herr Heinrich appeared, a welcoming look wreathing his pudgy face. "Come with me," he told them in French, and headed up the outside steps to the second floor. "I have two rooms. One for the children, and one for you."

✦⟫⟫⟨⟨⟨✦

HANS HEINRICH WAS an accommodating host. Throughout the evening and into the wee hours, he brought up hot water, broth, and cloths that Liesel could use to minister to Nikky.

Dirk had taken Katrin down to the great room, where they had their supper. Liesel's little sister was well satisfied afterward, and happily went to bed in the adjoining room. At once, Dirk left to find the local apothecary and brought back solutions of mint and chamomile for Nikky to sip.

But the boy's cough deepened and his fever rose. He tossed and turned upon the plush eiderdown until past midnight. Then, spent, he lay still. Liesel and Dirk took turns applying cool cloths to his forehead and bathing his limbs in cool water.

"Go to bed," Dirk whispered to her. "I will do this." She

would have refused, but he set his jaw. "I'll hear no objections."

Liesel left them and crawled into the soft comfort of the bed with Katrin. She fell into a dreamless sleep.

The clatter of other travelers walking the hall awakened her. She startled, unsure where she was. The small room seemed warmer than it should be, and through the tiny window above them, Liesel could tell the sun was high.

She rose, unsteady on her feet. A shiver ran through her and she wished she had a shawl. But Katrin still slept soundly, thank heavens. Liesel crept into the bedroom where Nikky lay. Beside him was Dirk, his arm around the boy's waist. In the night, Dirk had shared his body heat to warm her brother. Tears scalded her eyes, but she blinked them away.

She rushed to lean over Nikky to listen to his chest. His lungs were clearer this morning. She wanted to feel his forehead, but dared not wake him from his rest. However, the one she had awakened slowly smiled at her, drowsy with his own rest.

Thank you, she mouthed.

He lifted a hand as if to brush off his service. Then he shooed her back to bed. She made a motion that she wanted a drink. He put up his palm, then shook his head as if to say he would get that. When she opened her mouth, he raised his brows at her.

She bit her lips to hold in her laughter. Hands on her hips, she nodded and pointed toward the door.

He scowled at her in playful regard, then carefully lifted the quilt and left the bed. *You,* he pointed at her, then pointed toward the other room.

"Tyrant," she murmured, and scurried back to the warmth of the bed.

DIRK BROUGHT CREAMED oats, bread, jam, and tea for Liesel, but she was asleep when he returned. He did not wake her. Instead, he made himself comfortable in the only chair in the room and waited for Nikky and Katrin to awaken. It was after one in the afternoon when they roused.

He motioned for Katrin to join him in the hall. "I will get luncheon for all of us, and more tea and soup for Nikky. If Liesel wakes, help your sister to wash and refresh herself. She was up most of the night nursing your brother, and she needs you."

The girl looked worried, and was most eager to help. "I can make a new poultice for Nikky's chest if you think it would help him."

"It would. Thank you."

She rubbed her eyes, but rose to the task. "I know how Mama used to do it."

As they opened the door, Liesel coughed. Dirk shot a glance at Katrin.

She winced and whispered, "Liesel used to get sick like Nikky."

Alarm froze him. "Will you also make a poultice for Liesel? I will return with more food and tea."

He took the stairs down at a clip and entered the gathering room. It was crowded. Men, women, and children sat or milled about. All ate and drank. A fiddle player plucked at his instrument while his friend flexed his fingers over a piano and another struck chords on a concertina. At a nod to each other, they began an old drinking song. The guests took up the melody immediately. A few men stood, mugs in hand. The whole room burst into song.

"Du, du, liegst mir in Herzen. Du, du, liegst mir in Sinn…" You, *you live in my heart. You, you live in my mind.*

Dirk blew out a huge breath as he stood by the main barrels. He loved this song. It described his life now. Liesel lived in his mind and his heart, just as the lyrics said, and he would not let her down. He'd give her anything. If she suffered as Nikky had, he would do all in his power to save her. Tea, soup. Stew, bread, beer. Hot poultices now for her chest. She was worn with worry and care of Nikky. Worst of all, she worried about their safety and their future. He would not fail her.

He glanced around the large room filled with a few travelers and local inhabitants who clearly knew each other and liked to debate, all enjoying their beans and sausage with beer steins in hand.

But as his gaze swept over one set of friends, some familiarity had him going back to take another look.

Twenty feet away from him, a tall, broad-shouldered man with dark brown hair and even darker brown eyes locked his gaze with Dirk's. The fellow wore poor merchant's togs of faded gray wool and linen. The cap on his wavy black hair was old and the scarf around his throat was a dull brown. Despite his weathered complexion, he looked pale.

Dirk flinched at his recognition.

What is he doing here? How did he come here?

Dirk tipped his head to the man to indicate they should meet outside in the courtyard to talk.

"*Gutentag, Mein Freund,*" Dirk said to him in his native language as the man approached and grinned at him. "*Was bist du, herein?*"

Rainer, Crown Prince of Rittenburg, reached out, and the two men embraced. "I need to ask you what *you* are doing here, Mein Herr."

"The same as you." Dirk dared not speak his name out loud.

Rainer blanched.

Dirk nodded, and the two of them moved to the street corner, far from other ears.

Rainer tensed. "You flee the French?"

Chapter Twelve

"RAINER?" HE WAS a vision. Liesel rubbed her eyes and took a longer look at the handsome fellow standing next to Dirk. She marveled that this new visitor resembled their father. His height, his broad shoulders, and his long, lean physique presented a younger version of their father. Even his dark brown hair waved upon his brow just as their father's had. She struggled up on her elbows, but the room spun.

Rolf was already licking the long fingers of the man who appeared before her.

"Rainer?" she repeated.

"Yes, Liesel. I am here." He eased her down to the pillows and bent to put a kiss on her forehead.

But his tenderness could not kill her anger. She shot up, her head reeling. "You left them!"

Dirk rushed toward her and urged her back to the bed.

"No! No. You left them alone," she accused her brother. Katrin stood beside Rainer, her eyes wide.

"Liesel, forgive me."

"No. I won't. I won't." She shook her finger at him, but it wasn't enough.

"What's wrong?" Nikky stood on the threshold. "Rainer?" The little boy stood there in his nightshirt, blinking in wonder at

125

the tall, regal man who stood with Dirk.

Rainer held out his arms, and Nikky rushed into his embrace.

Liesel fumed and swung her legs over the side of the bed. She'd make certain Rainer…

What *did* she want her brother to do?

She stood and groped for the wall. Her knees gave out.

Dirk caught her tightly against him. His warmth, his strength, suffused her, and she turned into him and put one arm over his shoulder. "Tell him he failed."

Rainer stepped forward. "I should hold her."

"No." Dirk seared her brother with his gaze. She felt his objection to Rainer's bark and thrilled to it. What good had etiquette ever done for her? Or Dirk.

She burrowed into him and moaned. Dirk was no man to dissolve at her brother's ferocity. She smiled that he'd keep her in his hold.

"She's been ill, Rainer. The same thing as Nikky. She needs rest and quiet." He laid her down.

She lifted a hand to her brother. "Why do you come here?"

"A meeting with friends in the city," he murmured.

Why did he sound like he was talking to a child?

"Don't humor me."

"No, Liesel. I know the innkeeper." He threw her a small smile. "Don't worry, sweeting. I'll leave now."

"But…but… No, don't go." She'd not seen him in years, and they needed him. Her thoughts blurred one into another. "Mama would not want you to be here. The French…" she whispered, and licked her dry lips. "They will hunt you."

Rainer leaned close. "Never worry about me, my dumpling."

She sniffed. "I'm no dumpling, you cad."

"No, sweet girl," Rainer said as he ran a hand over her brow. "You are a beauty."

"Rainer." Liesel closed her eyes. They were too heavy, and she was so very tired. She shivered and huddled down into her eiderdown.

"Rainer," Dirk called. "Come with me. We must talk."

Liesel curled her knees to her chest as someone pulled the thick goose down quilt up to her chin. They could go. She had her older brother once more. She could sleep.

⊁⟫⟫⟨⟪⟪

"WHY ARE YOU here?" Dirk closed the heavy wooden door of the linen closet and faced Rainer. The air was humid, but filled with the smell of newly milled soap and lemons. Pink and green rays of light shone through the small stained glass window. The pink gave Rainer the aura of health he did not possess. Dirk had minutes to persuade him to leave.

"I came here to hide. The same as you, Fournier. Who knew you'd have my family with you?"

Dirk ignored his friend's anger. "A necessity. Liesel came to me from Ettenheim."

"Ettenheim? What on God's earth was she doing there?" No sooner were the words out of Rainer's mouth, he paled. "No. Tell me she was not with the Duke of Enghien!"

"She was. I do not know details. I have not asked. I doubt she will say. She considers his capture her failure." *Like me, she does not wear her failures lightly, and I do not blame her. But neither do I think less of her for them. I love her all the more for having tried.*

"But why come to you?"

Dirk threw his friend a look of rueful dismay. Rainer must not have learned much about his mission to save so many Germans from French clutches. He would not take time to reveal his own secrets, especially to Rainer, who could be captured and tortured himself. "She thinks I am reliable."

"I guess you are, to have come this far with them."

As a concession, it was small, but Dirk would not elaborate on his own expertise in the art of smuggling people to safety. But he could fill in a bit of Rainer's knowledge about his missing sister. "Liesel has been busy. The French know quite a bit about her activities. Before Ettenheim, she was in Strasbourg."

"Dear God! Why?"

Dirk fought a smile. "She was in Paris before that. Working in the kitchen of the French deputy minister of police."

"You do jest."

Dirk cast him a wide-eyed stare. "I wish."

"She worked for Vaillancourt?" Rainer cursed roundly in gruff German. "Why? *Why?*"

Dirk contemplated how Liesel's brother would take another shock. He decided this last bit would humble the man and give Liesel her just rewards. "You can imagine why, Rainer."

"Nooo. She's an agent?"

"She knows much," Dirk said with an inhale. He'd not give away any details of her connections in London. "And has learned much. She's not suffered too much, but she came to me because she expected the French would abduct your brother and sisters to use as ransom to persuade you to surrender to them. She came to me for aid. And as you can see, I gave it." Dirk needed information himself. "Now, you tell me. Why do you hide here?"

Rainer breathed heavily. "I was discovered last night in the city."

As I feared. "And had to flee?"

"I left my four men. We dispersed."

"None came with you here?"

"None."

That was a comfort. But not a guarantee of safety. "What happened?" Had Rainer or his men gotten into trouble in Koblenz?

Rainer's jaw twitched. "Vaillancourt arrived in Koblenz last night."

"Far out of his usual territory, isn't he?" Dirk's sarcasm covered his terror. He paced to the window and back.

"Far from Paris. But I understand Fouché has elevated him to deputy minister over his political police."

Rainer's enemy was also Liesel's. Vaillancourt's reason to

leave Paris was direr than any Dirk had ever imagined. He squeezed his eyes shut. It could mean the deputy was here for both Rainer and his sister. "How many men does he have?"

"Twenty French soldiers. And ten gendarmes from his Paris garrison."

"So…thirty men?" Dirk ran both hands through his hair. Had Vaillancourt's agents followed them from Rittenburg? What had he missed along the road? Anything? Any sign? Anyone who tracked them? "Are you sure of the count?"

"My own men drank with his. Vaillancourt comes for me."

Dirk cursed beneath his breath.

"He wants me, Dirk. Me. Bonaparte killed Enghien for fear of a Bourbon uprising. Bonaparte fears a German uprising against him, led by me. So I am next."

"And Liesel, too."

"What? Why?"

"She worked in Vaillancourt's kitchen in Paris. I don't know for how long, but somehow she was discovered for who she was…and she fled east. First to Ettenheim. Recently, to me."

Rainer's pale eyes lit with fear. "She was always so stubborn, and too bold for her own good."

Hell, what did it matter how or why Liesel had secured a position in Vaillancourt's household? If the deputy minister and his contingent were here, he was after Rainer or Liesel or both. What a prize the two crown royals of Rittenburg would be.

"If you know Vaillancourt is here, why are you still here?" Dirk asked. "Drinking openly in the great room is not exactly wise."

"One of my men was shot. I brought him across the river to Herr Heinrich because I knew he would take care of him. I was having a drink, and then Heinrich was going to hide me. Little did I think I would find you and Liesel here with Nikky and Katrin." Rainer sank against the door.

Dirk saw now the extent of his friend's pallor. He was a big man, broad shoulders, long legs, but he looked strained. He'd lost weight. His travels had not treated him kindly.

"Liesel is ill. You saw it yourself. She needs a bed, comfort, good food. We have only just saved Nikky from death."

Rainer's blue eyes darkened. "Nikky was ill?"

"Very. Until Liesel recovers, I will not chance moving her far. Which means—"

"I must go."

Dirk nodded. "Do you have other friends?'

Rainer rolled his eyes. "Oh, I do. Hundreds. Thousands!"

"Choose one, as fine as Hans."

He nodded. "I will."

"Then find someplace to recover your own health."

"Never worry about me. Save the others. For that, I am indebted to you."

"Never. I am honored she asked me."

Rainer looked him over with narrowed eyes. "You care for her."

Not a question, but a statement. "I do."

"Even to take her to your country where they may come to arrest you."

"They need never know I was there."

"And if they do?"

"I will deal with that as it comes. My only task now is to see them all safely to my mother in Kent. She will rejoice to have the royal family of Rittenburg in her home."

"Your mother is still a lady-in-waiting to the queen?"

Dirk nodded. "Her most useful job, she says."

"Which may keep you from a dungeon."

"But not from public ridicule." Dirk preferred not to think of his possible prosecution. "I concentrate only on Liesel's happiness now."

Rainer put both hands to Dirk's shoulders. "If you love her, and she you, marry her."

A shimmer of delight winged through Dirk. To have Liesel forever in his life, in his bed, would be more grace than heaven should grant him. But reality stung. "I would never disgrace her so."

"You and I both know you did not ruin that woman."

Dirk scoffed. "Really? You think not?"

"I do. You are not a man to despoil a lady and leave her in disgrace."

"Rainer, my friend, you are one of two who believes that." His mother would crow to learn his friend the Prince of Rittenburg thought him innocent.

They embraced, the strong bond of friendship tying them to each other in spirit.

Rainer stuck two fingers in the coil of his worn scarf. "We must get out of here before we boil."

They locked gazes and laughed.

"Be swift," Dirk told his friend.

"Be smart," Rainer told him. "Some bright day, we meet again."

"Make a point of living that long, Mein Herr."

"*Javohl, Mein Freund.*"

Chapter Thirteen

D IRK RAISED HIS hand and put his ear to the door. Hearing no one about, he swung it open, peered into the hall, and motioned for Rainer to follow. The prince had already bidden *auf wiedersehen* to Nikky and Katrin, so he took the stairs down to the gathering room at a clip.

Dirk expected not to see his friend again for years.

If ever.

The words hung in Dirk's mind as he noted the sound of horses nickering in the stable yard. Rainer was away quickly.

Dirk hurried back to Liesel. She lay upon the bed, crumpled into a small, quivering ball. Her forehead and her hands were hot as summer sun.

He had to work harder to get her fever down. But a glance at the basin told him he needed more water to make compresses. He shook the teapot. He needed more of that, too. He called for Katrin to go down and fetch tea and something to eat.

A hand to Liesel's brow, he bent, and she stared up at him. Her stunning violet eyes were strained and glassy. "You're here."

"Always."

Her lips curved in a tremulous smile. "I want you near."

His heart twisted. "I must get more chamomile and mint at the apothecary. But I'll return at once."

Her fingers edged along the linen to take his hand. Her shoulders curled as if in pain. "I want no other man…"

He fought the urge to blurt out his own desire for her. But it would do neither of them any good. In such a fever, she would not remember the declaration, and he would not forget.

He secured the eiderdown to her throat. "Don't go away."

She had enough awareness of his jest to smile. Did she know how she touched him with words and deeds? He had to hope she never did.

He jogged down the stairs to the main room and saw no one about. That was odd. Where was Hans? Where were those townsfolk who usually came for their lunch and their steins of beer? Where was Katrin? The stable yard? The kitchens?

Alarm winging through him like a vulture, he headed for the kitchens.

Hans burst through the door to the cellars. "Mein Herr!"

"Where is my charge, Hans?"

"*Kommen Sie, bitte.*" Hans urged him to through the kitchen door. "Your little one is in the cellars."

"*Was ist los?*" *What's wrong?*

"Soldiers, French, are in the *platz*. Ten, says my daughter. They come this way."

"Which way did our visitor go?"

"South. As soon as one of my maids told me of the French, I took the children to the wine cellar. They think it a great adventure."

"I'm sure the fragrant angel's share alone will fill them with good spirits. But Hans, I must hide my lady and our little boy. And it should be…"

"Somewhere else. *Ja, Ich weiss.*" *I know.*

"Where?" Dirk asked himself more than Hans.

But the man stared at him with narrowed eyes. "The tunnels."

Dirk recalled the time he, Rainer, Ashley, and Appleby had played there as youths. The long, winding corridors were damp, moldy excavations completed in the time of the religious wars. A few of the passages ended in dead ends. Others meandered onward for a mile or two. Years ago, Hans had shown them three entrances. All were obscured by an overgrowth of vines and grasses. The tunnels were on Hans's property, had been for generations, and few went there, few knew of it, except his family. He had assured the men then that only his father and he knew the locations. Now, Hans explained only his wife and daughter knew them. "I recommend the main tunnel, Mein Herr. *Das Eishaus.*"

Precisely. The icehouse, built into the side of a hill, was a stone building of three concentric circles. Only the central one was of use. Inside, Hans and his wife stored supplies for the inn. Dirk recalled seeing wooden crates filled with seasonal vegetables and fruits, shelves with soft rounds of cheese, and chunks of ice they had seized with grappling hooks during the winter from a nearby lake.

Dirk bit down hard on his dislike of taking Liesel to such a place. She was so ill. So fevered.

But truly, if anyplace was safe from Vaillancourt's reach, it was a house deep in the woods obscured by the flourishing, green growth of centuries—and filled with ice.

Dirk took the stairs two at a time, Hans right behind him. Dirk warmed only at the sight of Liesel resting. He hated to disturb her, but he inched down the bed covers and scooped her into this arms.

She tucked her nose into the curve of his throat. "Why?"

He fought for words to sustain her. "We go on an adventure."

"Ah. My knight."

He put his lips to her brow. He burned for her. "My princess."

"Cold."

"I know," he said as he took the stairs with his darling burden. "I'll get you warm soon enough."

Waiting at the landing, Hans held one small candle in a silver lamp. Nikky, with his breeches on now, held another. Katrin stood beside him. Hans tipped his head toward the servants' stairs down to the kitchens, the pantry, and the wine and beer cellar.

As they approached the large double doors, Dirk paused. "Perhaps it is best for the two children to go to the other tunnel."

Hans agreed, and the four of them hurried down the dank corridor.

If Liesel and Dirk were found in the icehouse, it would be best if Nikky and Katrin were not with them. The French would have to think hard to gain their hostages. For two years, Dirk had not made it easy for them. He would not start now.

But the tunnel was damn long. Liesel was a tall woman, slight of build, but even so, carrying her in the pitch-black corridor wore on him. He had to stop twice to catch his breath.

At last, they reached a dead end of one tunnel and Hans paused. Then he pushed aside a tall wooden shelving that opened to a hole in the wall, and disappeared down a new corridor.

Liesel writhed in his arms. "I am cold."

"You'll be warm soon." What else could he do but lie? "I am with you."

She moaned, and he grieved with her.

"Come." Hans appeared and led the way around to a scarred wooden door that looked as if it had been hacked with axes and charred with torches.

Hans closed the door behind them and led the way up a flight of limestone stairs through another door. Inside a true building now, the air was clean and crisp.

"The first ring," Hans informed him. At ten more paces, another door appeared. "This one is weighted with stone between the wood panels. It takes me a while to slide it open. Come, sit here with your lady."

Dirk sank to a ledge carved from the stone. His thoughts swam with his friend's words. *Your lady.*

He shifted her in his arms and allowed his limbs relief from his burden.

In response, Liesel trembled in her fever. This business of hiding from Vaillancourt's men did her no good. One day he'd have recompense for this pain the man had caused her. One day…

The scraping of the weighted door upon the stone threshold had Dirk turning to marvel at Han's strength.

"You must tell me how you can do that so easily," he told his friend as he got to his feet.

"When you move mountains once a week, you become more capable each time." Hans closed the door upon them. "Only one more."

This door, Dirk could see from his vantage. It looked as if it had been recently replaced. Planed and clean of mold, this door seemed nonetheless as heavy as the previous. But Hans bent to his chore to move it open.

Dirk stood with Liesel in his arms. The cold air inside whirled through the door, forming clouds that met his nostrils and made him wince.

He strode inside with her. Two steps in and the true meaning of "icehouse" blasted Dirk's skin with a thousand frigid knives.

Liesel reared her head, her eyes wide at the assault of cold.

Hans murmured that he had shawls. He strode to an ancient, domed bombé trunk and extracted two. "They are not thick, but they'll help keep you warm. We put them around our shoulders when we work here."

Dirk strode to one of two chairs in the room and sat down with Liesel in his lap. "You need more than this."

"Ja, but we leave what we bring and take what we want quickly. Please listen to me now."

Dirk worked at covering Liesel with the wool shawl. "You will leave us."

"I will. If the French come to the inn, they will want to speak to the proprietor. My wife can hold them off for only so long. My daughter is too young to manage soldiers or gendarmes."

"I understand. Go."

Hans took a large flask from the shelves behind him and grabbed two silver mugs from another below. "Schnapps. Drink it. There is not much here to eat except raw potatoes and carrots we cut days ago. No cream or cheese, I'm sorry to say. We took it all into the kitchens yesterday."

"I'm grateful for the schnapps, Hans. Although I hope you can return before I pass out in a stupor." Dirk regarded Liesel. "I cannot feed her spirits for her fever."

Hans raised a finger. "I have ice!" He spun away to the far wall and took down an earthen pitcher.

Dirk could hear the crystals sloshing against the pottery as Hans brought it to him.

"Pour, will you please?" He was eager to give Liesel a drink, and he could use some, too. He flexed his fingers. "My hands are numb."

Hans had a grin on his fleshy face as he filled two small mugs with icy water. "All right! Now I go." Peeking back into the room before he closed the door, he said, "All will be well."

Dirk smiled to reassure his friend, who had done everything he could to help hide them.

Now he had to ensure Liesel survived this wickedly cold room.

"Here you are, my darling." He tried to get her to part her lips for a sip of the ice water. But she scowled and turned her head away. "Please, you must drink."

"No." She swatted at his hand. "Cold in here."

"I know, sweetheart, but we must stay here only for a little while."

She wrapped one arm around his torso and nestled into him. "You're warm."

With you in my arms, in this ridiculous frozen hideaway, yes, I am.

"I want to crawl inside you."

He shut his eyes. Curled her close. "I know."

"Would you—?" She let her head loll back against his arm.

Her stare held madness and feverish desire.

"What?" He was taken, enchanted by the ramblings of a lady so ill, she knew not what she said. He smiled as he threaded his fingers through her rich golden hair.

"Would you have me?"

"Yes, darling." Was he losing his mind to admit such a thing? What did it matter what he had or hadn't said? Rainer had noticed Dirk cared for his sister. Katrin and Nikky had mentioned it. They all had eyes to see. "Were we free, I'd have you."

"Not like him."

Him. The one who'd abused her.

"Iceberg," she muttered.

Dirk twitched. Her reference, in any other circumstance, would have made him laugh. But here, freezing as they were, for her to make a mash of her intended's name only fired his anger. "He won't ever have you."

She whimpered and snuggled into his care. "He hit me," she murmured.

"Oh, sweetheart." He took her chin between his thumb and forefinger. She focused on him as she weaved in her delirium. "I am so sorry. I will kill him for you."

"Oh, good," she said. "I knew you would. I love you," Liesel whispered, a broken sound of despair.

With his mind so full of anguish, he had almost missed her words. Hell, he was an idiot to discuss such vital matters with a severely ill woman. Still, he must, mustn't he? What she remembered, if anything, of this conversation in this dungeon of ice had to be his objection to her sweet regard.

"Oh, my darling, no. I am no man to love."

"You are," she cried, and kissed his throat, his jaw, then put two fingers to his lips. "You are my knight, Dirk Fournier. Mine."

Hot tears stung his eyes. But he urged her close to him and fought his desire to kiss her back. Instead, he silently cursed his struggle and arranged her thin shawl between them. No fabric, no layers of iron or brick or stone, could bar his heart from loving her. Only his ethics. They—essential to his integrity as they were—became more fragile every minute with her so close, so dear.

How could he clear his name and take her to wife? Employ his list. His damn list.

He knew not how many minutes later, but Hans finally reappeared and opened the door to freedom and warmth. Dirk carried Liesel back to their room, their bed, where he climbed in beside her to share his body heat and calm her from bouts of chills. By dawn, she was still, curled against him—and cool.

By that afternoon, Vaillancourt's raiding party had left the town, headed south. Rumor said they tracked Rainer. Dirk arranged for the four of them to leave Koblenz the next night in a hired traveling coach going northeast.

Chapter Fourteen

THAT NIGHT, THEY traveled to a tiny village ten miles east before he settled them in an inn. Dirk hated to prolong their journey, but he continued to fear that the French would come across the Rhine. True, Vaillancourt was said to have taken his contingent south, but that was no guarantee he would not send others under his command into German territory. Dirk had to avoid Bonn and Cologne and any towns on the way to Amsterdam. The Belgian provinces and the Dutch were now allies of France, and he would not risk their lives by going there.

Nor would Dirk call upon any rulers whom Liesel knew to take them in. Those men might be persuaded by the French to hand over the likes of the Crown Princess of Rittenburg, who had worked against them. Neither did they enter any towns Liesel had been through on her previous journeys. If she knew a shopkeeper or an innkeeper, or even the local magistrate or the cleric, Dirk skirted the town, even if it meant that added another day or two to their trip to the sea.

In reality, this diversion toward Hanover and the sea meant they would travel another month at least to reach a northern port. The deeper route into German territory was safer.

Yet each day was a weary trail of hours in old, uncomfortable coaches drawn by slow horses. Liesel uttered no complaints. She was setting an example. The children grumbled and complained about the food, the beds, their dirty clothes. The dog was the happiest soul, content simply to be with those he loved.

Eating the meals cooked by innkeepers was not so bad, but the beds—short and old, cold and thin—were the worst problem. At least, after weeks of this, they were all healthy. What saved their journey was mild, sunny weather—and jovial company.

Dirk, however, had his own challenge. Preserving his sanity became a minute-to-minute exercise. Duty kept him occupied during the day—changing carriages, arranging nights at coaching inns, assuring the other three that they were safe, secure, that no one followed them. But sitting across from Liesel for endless hours, he found himself learning the fullness of who she was, hearing tales of her childhood, her father's instructions in democratic rule, and her love of her land and her people.

He understood those values. He lived them himself. Then, for the first time in many years, he heard himself sharing stories of his youth, his friends—one of whom, Tate Cantrell, she had met that first night she burst into his house in Karlsruhe.

Long days of idle conversation informed him of more and more who she was, and his admiration for her grew. The revelation of her character, strong and resilient, fused with his reverence for her beauty. That first time he'd seen her, he concluded she was the loveliest woman he'd ever beheld. True then, but it was doubly so now. Her vivacity and her wit stunned him. His desire to possess her was a challenge in the confines of a tiny carriage in the presence of two children.

But now, as they gazed upon each other all through each day, she also showed him, by act and deed, her growing desire for him. The way she regarded him, admiration in the tip of her head. Yearning in her large amethyst eyes. Consternation in her pout when he withdrew his hand. He dared not touch her more than necessary—he would not cross the boundary of propriety, even though at night, their every mood changed.

His days were an elegant misery of travel wrapped in an

electric attraction to her every word, her every look. His nights were a living hell. Always, everywhere they stopped to rest in an inn at night, the two of them shared a bed. It was necessary. The establishments were always small, the rooms few. He would insist upon two beds, but often what they were offered was one room with one eiderdown or a pile of hay. Always attempting to remain a gentleman, he had proclaimed at the start of their journey that he would sleep on the floor. Liesel would not have it.

"I cannot do that," he began one night.

She put two fingers over his lips. "I will not let you sleep on the cold, hard wood. Come lie down with me here, or I will lie down with you there."

He went. Lured by necessity to sleep and desire to be so near her, God help him, he went.

Flat on his back, he would start the night. Staring at the ceiling, tossing one way, then another, he rotated like a chicken on a spit. His thoughts wandered to how he would take her, strip her of her simple cloak and gown, unlace her corset, and trace the elegant lines of her arms and her hips and her thighs. How he was to fall asleep, he could not fathom. But he would, granting himself few hours of nothingness. Still, he'd awaken in the middle of the night—and find Liesel flush against him, one arm, one leg over him, her lips a temptation away.

He'd disentangle himself and fight to sleep again. But often in the morning when he awakened, she was snuggled close, too near, too dear. And he had to find what restraint he could summon.

Often, that was so very little. He'd not had a woman in so very long. More than a year, even before Liesel had stormed into his bathing room in Karlsruhe. He'd vowed celibacy after the disaster in London with Alicia Sedgwick. Not because he felt guilty. No, he had no guilt that Alicia and the man who accused him of ruining her had been successful. On the contrary—he found it useful to behave in such a way that no one could accuse him of being a scoundrel. Since then, he had broken his promise to himself three times. Each time, he had carefully chosen and paid well for a suitable companion for a few hours. But now, in this time of desperate need to flee and survive, he was eaten alive by the desire to touch and caress, to adore and claim the one extraordinary woman whom he could never take as his own.

And he knew that if he broke, if he weakened and pulled her to him in the night, if he put his arm around her or lifted his leg to draw her to him, he would make such sweet love to her that he'd never forget it. Nor would he ever pardon himself the crime.

Once home, in England, Liesel would return to her place in Society. She would go to her control agent in London, and share where she'd been and how she had escaped the clutches of René Vaillancourt. She would take her two siblings and create a new life for herself.

He would have no part of that. Society had cast him out long ago. They would not accept him back into the fold. To them he was damned, marked by lies of two more powerful than he. He would return to the Continent. Hide himself away from the French. Reconnect with Scarlett's agents, who were merchants, clerics, and civic leaders. He'd establish himself with runners who would relay messages across the land and sea, back to London and Scarlett and those in government who needed to know everything from numbers of soldiers to movement of arms.

He had a purpose in this life. It had fulfilled him for years. But purpose would never equal love. He knew it, and felt the hollowness of his future in his bones.

But what could he do to change that?

His list, his cursed list of remedies, sprang to mind. Each night, each day.

Torture left him only when he imagined how to confront his accusers. To kill them was impossible. To ruin them was necessary.

But how?

And if he could, if he did, to what end? None. Liesel would

not be able to have him as her husband. She was betrothed. A crown princess. He was a baron. British, at that. A man sullied, he would never be her equal. He was unworthy.

Irredeemable.

But he had to try, didn't he?

THREE WEEKS OUT of Rittenburg, they reached a small port outside Bremen. This was Hanoverian territory once owned by George III. Now it was aligned with the French, but they were few and weak here. The hearty merchants and fishermen of this bustling area near the waters of the North Sea avoided the French in the Channel at all costs.

Liesel sighed, thrilled to be safer here and about to depart the Continent. As their coach approached an inn on the harbor, the children squirmed to be set free. Nikky clapped. Katrin squealed as their carriage came to a stop and they all climbed out.

Liesel accepted Dirk's hand, then hooked her arm through his. Such little touches he allowed her more each day. Their nights spent so close broke more barriers to their everyday ease with each other.

Nikky stood, his mouth open at sight of the huge ships at anchor. He caught Dirk's free hand. "Please, sir, might we stay here tonight and walk around the city?"

Rolf lifted his furry head in expectation.

"I don't know if it's safe to do that," Dirk replied. "Let's go in, and I will ask the owner if it's wise."

Shown to a clean room on the topmost floor of the guest house, they washed their faces and hands and went down to dinner. The roast turning on the spit in the huge fireplace had them all licking their lips in anticipation.

Full of meat, potatoes and apples, they sat on wooden benches and grinned at each other.

"How much longer, sir?" Katrin asked Dirk.

"Not long. Depending on the weather, we may be in England within days."

Liesel recalled her own tempestuous crossings and said nothing to refute him.

"And then what?" Katrin asked.

"We travel to London. That may be two or three days too, depending on where we land."

At that news, Nikky sulked.

Katrin pondered that with a frown, then folded her arms. "How many have you saved like us?"

"A few."

Liesel suppressed a smile. His modesty was wonderful.

"Did you accompany all the families to the coast?"

"No, only you." He grinned at both children.

But Katrin got the devil in her eye. "And how many ladies in distress have you saved?"

"Two."

"Were they princesses?"

"No."

"Did you like them as well as you like Liesel?"

He was solemn as he said, "No."

"How old are you?" This came from Nikky.

Dirk took a breath. This personal inquiry held a bit of surprise for him, judging by how he shifted on the bench. "Thirty-one."

"Liesel is twenty-three," Katrin offered.

Liesel held back a smile. Her sister was match-making—again. And Dirk knew it.

Katrin leaned toward him. "Have you ever courted a lady?"

Liesel was as much amused by her sister as she was embarrassed. "Katrin, please."

Dirk grinned at the young girl. "No, never."

"Why is that, sir? You are young and in good health. Handsome—and a baron, too. Do you not wish for a wife and children?"

He arched a long blond brow. "There has been no lady I have wanted."

"What if there were?"

"There was a scandal, Katrin. It shaped my life."

"It propelled you, here, yes, an immigrant among your mother's people. But even here, have you not found anyone you favor?"

"No."

"What power does a scandal wield in England?" Katrin demanded, sitting forward.

But Dirk sighed deeply, done with this subject. "A lot. Now, you will all please excuse me, as I need to find us passage out of here tomorrow."

⇒⟫⟪⇐

ROLF LOPED ALONG behind him. Dirk shooed him back to the others, but he continued to follow. And Dirk did need a friend who did not argue with him. "Very well, Rolf. Guard me from those who tempt me to barter over their prices, will you please?"

The dog smiled.

Dirk wished he could. But he had work to do.

He strode along the old wooden dock. He could not fault Katrin. Her questions were valid, her concern for her sister real. But he had to get out of there. He could not grant himself such high hopes.

The first man he met along the dock spoke good German. Dirk cared not what language he spoke; he wanted a quick way home. The fellow was leaving for Calais with the tide, and Dirk was ready to pay the fees when the captain looked down at Rolf. The animal, his usual buoyant self, wagged his tail.

The fellow pointed to the dog. *"Das Hund ist verboten."*

Forbidden? There was not a chance Dirk would leave this animal alone in this city, never to see his family again. He left the fellow where he stood.

"We'll find someone with more sense, eh, Rolf?"

At the end of the dock stood a sleek schooner, well kept and looking very seaworthy. When the sailor told Dirk his captain was below, Dirk took the gangway. The man who appeared was young—twenty, if a day.

His name was Jacques Durand, a Frenchman with inky-black hair, long as a pirate's, with an eye patch over one eye. He spoke French and German, even English, and Dirk liked the cut of him.

Durand told Dirk that Bonaparte was assembling his army for an invasion of Britain in the south, along the Normandy coast. The captain had sailed from there two days ago.

Dirk nodded, unhappy to hear that rumor verified. What was worse, the French fleet sat at anchor along the Channel. Their crossing, said Durand, would be a wide arc away from that naval line. Crossing this corridor to any English town could take five days or twenty. Their trip might be very long.

"I have one bunk, and it's small," Durand warned Dirk. "My hold is full, and you'll all sleep together. The children in the same alcove. But I'm pleased to have you."

"Even our Rolf?"

"Why not? All those we love must stay together, eh?"

When Dirk took them down to the berth and Katrin and Nikky saw that they were assigned hammocks, the two clapped. For them, the trip had suddenly taken a turn for the better.

They should have saved their optimism.

The open room resembled that of a ship of the line, though this was smaller—*much* smaller, drafty, and damp. Dirk flinched at the nightmare this crossing would be.

The sleeping alcove was tiny. The only bunk was long, able to accommodate a man of regular height. Not one six feet, two inches. Two hammocks swung from the wooden beams that crossed the rafters.

Dirk set his jaw. He'd spent the past weeks trying to keep his hands off Liesel. Yet at every new city, every new inn or coach, at every table, and now in this godforsaken Channel crossing, he would, of necessity, be near her. His arms at night reaching for her. His fingers finding the silken skin of her nape, the line of her throat, the curve of her firm thigh.

"This is the last temptation," he swore. It had to be.

He stomped up the steps, growling to himself about his failures.

When he reached the deck, Liesel strode toward him.

Two men who had boarded behind them argued with Durand. They spoke German with a French accent.

"You said we were going to London," one argued with Durand. "Now you say Yarmouth."

"I predict what I can, *monsieurs*. A storm can destroy our course. Worse, so can a skirmish with a French man of war. I cast off in an hour. Stay if you wish to cross. Leave if you don't."

"Our fees, please." One man put out his palm.

"*Certainment*," Durand grumbled as he reached inside his thick wool coat. "*Adieu*."

"Yarmouth. North of London?" Liesel turned her back on the captain as she faced Dirk. "More delay?"

He led her a few paces from the others. "Necessary to avoid the French on patrol in the Channel and a storm. This will not be a pleasant crossing."

She sighed in resignation. "I have never sailed the Channel and kept my breakfast. I don't need it now, with as much as we need to be free."

How could he do without her? She rallied at every point. "Let me tell you ten thousand times how I admire you."

"Don't be daft, sir. I do what is necessary." She riveted him with the sweet regard in her gaze. "Just as you do."

He could not stop himself, and took both her hands and kissed her fingertips. For the thousandth time, he wished he could have her lips. But he pushed desire away. "After this, I promise the most elaborate traveling coach I can hire to take us to Fournier Park."

"Ah, yes. With seats wide as the sea."

He laughed. "And fat squabs fit for a princess."

She rolled her eyes. "She asks for nothing more."

"She deserves everything I can give her."

Her mellow regard paled as her desire flared and seared his bones.

She stepped nearer. "I will never be able to thank you enough for all of this."

"I ask nothing." Her heat drew him so close that he felt the contours of her breasts.

"I wish I could."

Her plea had him drawing backward. He sought some objectivity. "You won't praise me when you see the sleeping quarters. Bear in mind, I use that term loosely."

"Terrible?"

"Beyond compare."

She shivered. They were still so close that he felt her distress, and his hands went to her shoulders.

"The bunk is not worth the name. Katrin and Nikky find the hammocks fun. That is, if the rocking of the boat does not bring up their accounts."

She nestled against him. The move was novel and not wise. The children scrambled up from below and saw them. Nikky did not question their friendship, but Dirk had caught Katrin eyeing the two of them more often. He would not damage Liesel's character in the eyes of her family.

Yet for the world, their passport papers said they were man and wife. So she could stand here. He could draw her close, breathe in her lingering scent of lemon, and yearn to keep her. No one would tell them nay. Not today.

"At each new turn of this journey," she murmured, her cheek soft against his shoulder, "I need this more."

How many times had he declared their affections were not wise? That his attraction to her was not rational? That his desire for her was a passing fancy built of circumstance and proximity?

But he'd lied to himself.

And his entire life was built on truth.

This desire for Princess Elizabeth of Rittenburg was as impractical as it was fantastical.

He dropped a kiss to her forehead. How could he not? She was vibrant and strong, wild and determined to be free…and he wanted her more each hour. But he pulled back. "I apologize. That will not happen again."

She looked as if she'd dissolve into thin air before him. "I don't promise I will not say the same again."

"Please, Liesel."

"Are there so many women you've had that you can refuse one who desperately needs your arms and lips and body as her own?"

"No." He jerked aside to clutch the ship's rail.

"Are they so available to you that I am not a temptation?"

"You are every bright lure a man could want."

"And you resist with every word. And yearn with every look. Every kindness."

"You are so far above me."

She let out a laugh. "A princess without a land—without a home, without money or influence? A woman who ruined herself?"

He whirled and gripped her. In the act, he brought her full against him. The press of her lithe body was a nightmare that sent him into a hell filled with the golden aura of all that she was to him. "I am your escort. Only that."

She shook back her unbound hair, and in her violet eyes was a prayer. "Can you not be my friend?"

"Yes, that."

"Nor my lover?"

"No. Never. You know it to be true."

"Do I?"

"We return to England, and the queen will find you a different man to marry. One you'll like, even love."

"I've already found him myself."

He glared at her. "One with a home and family you can be proud of."

"I'm proud of you."

"No. You must not be."

She sighed and put a hand to his heart. "You may not say you love me, but this"—she burrowed her hand beneath his waistcoat to his shirt—"this beats wildly. I know it is for me. But you are stubborn. Such a pity. You waste so much time, my darling man."

He stepped toward her, ready to gather her to him, take her, kiss her, taste the depths of her.

But she inched backward. "You have no idea how patient a woman can be." She tilted her head and smiled serenely at him. "I can wait. I will hate it. But I can wait. How long will you hold out?"

She tsked, then walked away to gather her brother, sister, and old, wet Rolf, and shoo them down the steps to the ungodly quarters.

⇥⟫⟩✕⟨⟪⇤

THROUGH WIND AND rain, storm and thunder, each night Dirk and she shared the cramped wooden bunk.

There was little choice how to position their bodies. They'd learned how to lie on other beds, how to sleep conveniently close, slumbering in each other's surrender to the tiny space.

But on this small schooner navigating a raging sea, their challenge to sleep together became a battle. This was to be their last span of hours together before they landed in England and headed to Fournier Park along the southern coast. With that looming over them, they gazed at each other as they took to the ridiculously tiny berth. They slept in their clothes, in the thick layers of their coats. The layers provided an insulation to the desire that in the night drew them instinctively into each other's embrace. Dirk understood in his heart that what they did together, how they lay together, would be the greatest gift they gave each other—and the final one.

THEIR MISERABLE CROSSING of the North Sea took seven days and nights. The storm and the French had them meandering north, south, and west.

"Tomorrow, we should reach Yarmouth," Durand told them.

Liesel stepped down into their alcove as the sun lowered to the glassy sea's horizon, feeling her heart clamp with sorrow. This was the end of her time with Dirk. Never to be duplicated. Ever to live her memory.

Dirk had stayed above, talking with Durand on deck. Nikky and Katrin had followed Liesel down, climbing into their hammocks. Excited that tomorrow this torture was over, they, as children could, slept deeply at once.

Liesel huddled into her wool pelisse and took her place carefully on the bed. Sorrow rushed through her like a tidal wave. She knew not how long it would take to travel from Yarmouth to Kent, but it had to be days, a week at most. That meant she would lose Dirk soon, never to regain him. So when he came and quietly, deliberately arranged himself along the arcs and planes of her body, she lay still. Not even a breath between them.

He took her hand and squeezed it against his thigh. It was more than he had ever done as they lay together. More than she'd expected tonight. And so, in the still black night, she slid nearer.

She felt his every inhalation, her own deep, soft. She smelled him, his skin sleek and musky. She snuggled nearer and dared to taste him. He was all man, his arm going around her, enveloping her, absorbing her into him as she dipped the tip of her tongue into the crevice behind his ear, along his throat, down to the hollow and his heart.

There she counted the beating of his blood, growing louder, throbbing against her lips.

She lifted one of his hands from her tangled hair and nipped the pads of his fingertips. He caught a swift breath and let her nuzzle his palm. His wrist was her favorite, his pulse pounding against her mouth. She nudged away his sleeves. The fine hair covering his forearm was like silk, the crook of his elbow a fine enchantment.

And there was the span of his chest. Broad, lean, and sculpted. She could push back on one elbow and admire it in the shards of moonlight fracturing the tempest-filled night. Here too, he had a dusting of hair, coarser than on his arms, but a mass she buried her nose into, imbibing how his ribs expanded with appreciation and surprise at her caresses and her pleasure.

One leg over his thighs told Liesel his delight in her raged through him. She could easily hover over him, encourage more, take more, but dropped her forehead to his chest and stayed her desires.

He inhaled, sank his fingers into her hair, and brought up her head. In the stark rays of light, she saw his torment. "I cannot take you only for one hour, Liesel. I would have to have all of you."

She knew his strength, his ethics, his morality would not permit him.

The next sound in the room was her gasp of heartbreak. He would not have her. Would not take her. How could she show him she did not care about tomorrow? Or England? The queen? His ragged reputation?

She knew he did not denigrate hers. He loved her for it.

And that fact alone made her halt—and stare at him.

Then, with the knowledge stuck firm in her mind that he did love her, she promised herself she would find a way to remove some of those barriers.

She rolled off him, curving her body along the strong planes of his. One arm around his chest, she snuggled against him.

He accepted her, cradling her close as the two lovers they

were in spirit, if not yet body.

But she would work for that. In England, she would ask for an audience with the queen. Not ask, but notify. That was what she would do. No one would drag her to an altar. She'd proven that once before when the queen's equerry had come, lied to her, and tried to trick her into going to Hanover Square Church.

She'd need money. Some. She hoped she had some left from her allowance in London banks from two years ago. To save whatever was left, she would economize. First, she would cancel the lease on her little Hanover Square house. She also would have to verify if Becker could still get her allowance into London through Rothschild's bank. With Bonaparte on the advance into Germany, the Frenchman could disrupt finances. She'd seen him bungle his own country's, degrading its value and ignoring financiers' pleas for stability.

Of course, she'd have to go to her contact at the Foreign Office and notify him of her arrival, tell him the tale of the woeful conditions in Northern Europe.

Lord Carlisle, a shrewd politician and agent, would welcome her appearance. His assistance to set her up in Paris had been vital to her masquerade there, although he'd had no influence on her entrance to René Vaillancourt's household as a kitchen maid. That little deceit was her own doing. But she was that assured her intelligence had reached Carlisle through the efforts of two women. One was a widow who worked as a governess to a French naval officer. Giselle Laurent had run Liesel's information through a lady who traveled the Loire River and Normandy up to Calais.

She smiled to herself in the dark of night. She had opportunities to rid herself of royal duties. She might never change her reputation as a crown princess of bad behavior. She cared not what the *ton* thought of her—and her reputation in England mattered not at all to Dirk.

He knew who she really was. And he loved her as she was. He need speak no words to verify her belief. His every action declared it. His reluctance now to take her completely to him proved it.

In the same vein, if she could not illustrate in words what she intended, she would show him by her actions.

What worth were mere sounds when deeds were the music of love?

On a deep sigh, she placed her lips to the hollow behind his ear and kissed him there.

She would tell him she loved him…and more when she was done.

Chapter Fifteen

Fournier Park
Kent, England
June 3, 1804

LIESEL STRAIGHTENED HER stiff back and rolled her shoulders. Her bones were not the only bits that needed fresh air and exercise. Her caged desires did, too. In the last six days since the four of them had disembarked Jacques Durand's schooner in Yarmouth, she had done nothing but yearn minute by minute for the end of this tiresome journey. Convincing Dirk to admit he cared for her would not be easy. Persuading him to do more, to spend his life with her, would be nigh unto impossible.

She could fix only so much. Her own status in Society was irredeemable, but she cared not for it. Fixing *his* status in Society was beyond her ability. But she could offer a solution for both, if he'd consider it. If he cared enough to make a life with her. If she could count on all the things she'd learned about him. His love of freedom. His love of others. His regard for children, her siblings, his friends…and her reputation. He might consider going to the United States, far from the madness of Europe and war. The idea was a wild one, but then, nothing was ever as inspiring as the promise of a new frontier.

Yet even that seemed a weak solution to their problem when they bought a newspaper outside London, and the main story stated that the French Senate had declared Bonaparte Emperor of the French. Liesel could see how it rankled Dirk that the little Frenchman grew in power and status. She paused to pray for the health and safety of her brother Rainer and her sister Mara. But here in England, she had to find some joy for herself. Each day, she promised herself the stamina to do that.

So as they rounded the circular drive up to Dirk's beloved Fournier Park, Liesel smiled at the beauty of it. She rejoiced that they'd escaped Bonaparte. Here in the temporary refuge of his country home, she would face her last chance to capture from Dirk any sign they could be together. Her time to do that here would be short. He'd told her so. How many days that was, she could probably count on her fingers. She had a few ideas how to change his mind. None of them involved any logic. Only passion. That he cared for her, she did not doubt. But would he agree to leave not only Kent and his mother, but also his work on the Continent?

Their coach idled. The huge, E-shaped mansion loomed above them. The groom jumped down from his perch and opened their door. It was time to change her actions. Time to make the life for herself that she now desired with all her heart.

The four of them seemed to take a huge breath, almost in unison. Even Rolf panted, viewing his new home. They mounted the wide portico, two giant stone lions snarling at them from pedestals on either side.

A liveried servant in midnight-blue and gold braid yanked open the wide front door of the whitewashed Elizabethan brick-and-stone house. "My lord? My lord?" he queried, shocked, not believing his eyes as he tried to adjust his wire-rimmed glasses. "Sir? Is that you?" he asked over and over as he surveyed their ragtag group.

"Jameson!" Dirk strode forward to grasp the older fellow's hand. "How are you? Well, from your looks, sir. I am so pleased to see you!"

"Aye, aye. And you, my lord. And you. My, my, we are...

You are… Hmm. All tired, hungry. Here, yes, here! And we are thrilled…thrilled, my lord." Jameson wiped tears from the corners of his watering eyes. "You are well? Yes? Oh dear. How are you here, sir? We had no letter. No word."

"No, Jameson. My apologies. I was in a hurry and expected we'd arrive before any messenger could give you adequate notice."

Actually, they had arrived in Yarmouth, well north of London, but, traveling south as Herr und Frau Schmidt with their children, Dirk had avoided the City. He presumed his mother was at home in Kent or with the queen at Windsor. Wherever she was, he would find her before he left England.

Dirk had not wished anyone to note that Baron Fournier had returned home. As for seeing Scarlett Hawthorne, he would report to her offices when he did go to London. In ordinary times, he would have called upon his friends, Lords Ashley and Ramsey. One of his runners had told him that both men and their wives were leaders of London Society. Of Appleby's fate, Dirk had been apprised by another of his colleagues who worked in Munich. Tate and the woman who had been with him that night last June were married, living in his estate in Norfolk. While tempted to stop at Tate's as they passed through Norfolk, Dirk had avoided that too. He had so little time to share with anyone. What energy he had, he would devote to Liesel and her two charges.

Dirk went on to his butler, "We are, as you can see, in need of everything in this world. Baths, clothes, luncheon, sunshine."

"Aye, my lord. And you shall have it. As well as your guests." The butler smiled at Nikky and Katrin. "We've not had youngsters here in many years, but it will be good. Very good."

"Indeed, it will be. My dear"—Dirk turned to Liesel with a grin—"allow me to present to you my butler and man of all that matters in this household, Mr. Jameson. Sir, this is Crown Princess Elizabeth of Rittenburg, her sister Princess Katrin, and brother Prince Nicholas."

The poor old man was agog, his funny little glasses sliding

down his nose. "My. My. You have had a time of it," he said as his gaze swept over their dismal apparel and fidgety forms. "Come, come! We will have you to rights in no time. What first? Food? Drink? Baths?"

Liesel closed her eyes and drank in the kindness around her.

"Luncheon, first, I do believe, Jameson. That gives you time to arrange rooms for our guests and baths. We also need something nourishing for our furry friend here. His name is Rolf, and scraps from Cook will serve him well."

Jameson bent to Rolf. "I shall have good things for you, fine sir. And I would think your two friends here"—he grinned at the children—"would like a bit of ice. Strawberry sound good, does it?"

Nikky shifted from one foot to the other and said in good English, "Oh, please, Mr. Jameson, sir. That would be wonderful."

Katrin licked her lips and nodded.

Dirk regarded Liesel. "Does that sound appropriate?"

"It does, sir," she said, offering her best English accent.

"I'll just pull the bell for a footman, and a maid can take the children to the kitchen for those ices. Do you have luggage, my lord?" Jameson took a glance at their carriage, still standing in the drive.

"A few small valises." Dirk spun to regard the footman and their coachman. "I am most grateful for their speed and kind agreement to bring us here so safely. We picked them up this morning in Tonbridge. Jameson, please see to their accommodations for the evening, and do give them a greater measure of my gratitude."

The two men who stood in the yard overheard, pulled the brims of their hats, and murmured their thanks.

"I want them to stay the night in the stables. They have charged the horses and nigh unto broken the axles to get us here. We were so eager and so tired. We've been on this journey since the dawn of time."

"Of course, sir. Yes, yes." Jameson clasped his hands over and over. Yet it was clear that he could not believe his eyes that his master stood before him. Even the sight of his guests did not compare to the wonder of regarding Baron Fournier. "You are a sight, if I may say so, my lord. Whatever you need is yours."

"Is my mother here, Jameson?" The yearning in Dirk's rough voice struck a poignant note in Liesel's heart. "I long to see her."

"My lord, I regret to tell you that your mother is in London."

"Oh. I had hoped she'd be here." He looked around the foyer as if he could not absorb enough of the abode where he had once lived and loved and passed his hours in childhood's blithe abandon. He seemed to grow taller, more serene, at peace to be among the people whom he had first loved, and they him.

A footman came scurrying around the corner and skidded to a halt. Surprised, he gave a small bow to all.

Jameson urged him forward. "Take the children down to Cook for ices, Herbert. Then return to me to get the master's and his visitors' bags."

As the servant disappeared, the butler regarded Dirk with concerned eyes. "Her ladyship left quickly last week, sir. But we can send a footman to notify her of your arrival. She will return straight away, sir. I know it."

"You are right. She will. I will have our man deliver a few messages to those in London. After dinner, I will compose those letters and give them to you."

"Excellent, sir." Jameson led them toward the large hall to the right and the grand double staircase. "Let's go up, shall we?"

Dirk put a hand to Liesel's back and led her forward. She felt relief that she would not meet Dirk's mother in her state of disarray. Instead, she wanted to draw in the grandeur of the blue Wedgwood walls, the cream-and-gold dome, the enormous family portraits, the marble and the gilt. She shared how Dirk imbibed satisfaction from the very air.

"When did my mother say she would return?" he asked Jameson.

"We have no notice, my lord."

"Problems in court?" But Dirk seemed not to care so much about the answer as their progress down the hall and into the splendor of a lavish salon, filled with settees and chairs all covered in a rainbow of flowered chintz. It was gay, inviting, and chaotic. But it created not a room, but a rambling English garden. With the large vases of roses and lavender, and daisies dotted with rosemary, the room had the fragrance of springtime and renewal.

The beauty of it took Liesel's breath away. She stood, looking around the circular room. Up, up, up her gaze traveled to the delights of cherubs dancing on the domed ceiling.

Even those in the frescoes were happy to be here. Happy to be home.

JAMESON PLACED LIESEL in a suite in the main wing. The butler had also provided four gowns, undergarments, shifts, and nightwear from the baroness's wardrobe. The lady's corset was too small for Liesel, and she rejected wearing it. Some things were best left undone.

"My lady has many clothes, Your Highness. She will be happy we provided for you in your hour of need."

Liesel accepted everything with gratitude. The baroness was as tall as her, if not as buxom. But the lady's color choices complemented Liesel's, and even the baroness's slippers fit her. Liesel went down to dinner that night in a purple sarcenet that matched the color of her eyes. In the intimacy of the cozy family dining room, she sat opposite Dirk, with Nikky and Katrin to either side.

They spoke of little things. The happy end to their journey. The walk Dirk had led them on to his tenants' cottages, and how happy those people were to greet their baron. Nikky had especially loved picking strawberries with a new friend of his, one of the tenants' sons. Katrin was simply happy to skip along in the sunshine.

When the children went off to bed, Dirk led Liesel into an adjacent room that was the small family salon. "There is a seamstress in the village," he told her as he stood before the ivory mantel of the fireplace. "I will have Jameson bring her to you tomorrow. For Katrin, too. We'll find a tailor for Nikky."

"For the children, that is kind of you. They need everything. But Dirk, I will not be here long enough for a dressmaker to finish her work."

"You need clothes."

"I can get them in London. I do have a house there. I am capable, Dirk."

Her tone had him tensing his jaw. "I want to see you settled."

"I am on familiar ground now. I can manage."

He hesitated, and she feared his next words.

"I will go to London tomorrow," he finally said.

So soon?

"I wrote this afternoon to my mother to tell her you are here. I am certain she will come as soon as she can. We need her to make your visit here acceptable."

Anger mixed with despair and whirled in her heart. "It's kind of you to care about that, Dirk, but I do not need it."

Her denial made him go stern with frustration. "You need the propriety. Rumors will fly that I escorted you from Rittenburg. It will get out, no matter our discretion. All of that reflects on you."

She stood her ground. "You cannot correct my reputation by calling forth your mother, nor by leaving so soon for London."

"Object all you want, my dear. But even Katrin and Nikky need the formality of good etiquette."

"I will take care of my brother and sister."

"Liesel, do not be rash. You need Society's acceptance."

That rocked her. He knew that what she really needed was him, free of his restraints. "You do not know me very well, do you?"

He paced toward the window. The night was dark, only a few stars twinkling above skimming clouds. "I value all that you are."

His tenderness could melt her down to nothing. But it meant little if he was determined to leave her.

She lifted her chin. "I too must go to London. Tell them I am alive and well."

"And see your friends in the Foreign Office?"

His sarcasm roiled her. If it was his effort to keep an emotional distance after all they'd been through, then she'd give him his own medicine. "Yes. Good people, they are. Doing fine work. Perhaps even resulting in useful results that you and yours might share with them."

He took the reprimand in silence.

She tried for a softer tone. "And you? You must see your own people."

He took a mighty inhalation and waved a hand. "Despite all, I will not leave you criticized here in England, at the mercy of the court."

She took it as insult that he would think of that first. "I am at no one's mercy. Especially not theirs."

He crossed his arms. How she loved him like that, so indomitable. "I know, but—"

"But you are wrong." She could live quietly in a village somewhere and make a life for herself and her brother and sister. She tipped her head. "I had a monthly allowance in Rothschild's bank from Herr Becker for many years. I expect the remainder is still there. Even if Becker cannot get money through Rothschild's banks to me, I will use what I have left to make a home for the three of us."

"Liesel, you may need more to survive. A home. Servants. Security. I will help you."

She set her teeth. If she could not have him, what did she want with his money and his help and anything to remind her of him? "I will not take your charity."

"It's not charity. I *want* to help you."

"I can make my way."

"Without a penny? How?" He grew red with frustration. "Will you go to the Foreign Office, to your agent, and ask for funds?"

"What a good idea," she purred.

"Absurd! They do not give money for no reason."

"You do not know my man."

"No? Who is it?"

"Lord Carlisle."

Dirk startled. "Clive Davenport?"

She could not care that Dirk knew him or knew of him. Carlisle was her contact, her agent, her friend. "A good man. Generous. Kind. Cool headed."

"He is. But he cannot support you with government funds."

"I will find a way. I've done it before."

Dirk narrowed his hazel eyes on her. "Stop this, Liesel. You cannot simply mention you were once Vaillancourt's kitchen maid."

"Then I will be someone's."

"Preposterous!"

"You underestimate me, my lord."

"Never."

Raw with travel, she was furious at his stubborn attempt to control her. "Let us speak plainly. Dirk, there are no more you can save. The Continent is closed to you."

He flexed his broad shoulders, looking in the depths of misery as he swung away.

She went to him and pressed her cheek upon his back. She would make her play. Her body pressed to his was all she had at the moment. And what were the odds she might win him over? She had no idea. "We could go to America. The new United States. We could all go. Leave this chaos and these fruitless wars."

He whirled in her arms. Shock lined his face, his bright eyes wide as he gazed down at her. "You would go so far?"

"To stay in Europe is madness."

"What of Rainer? Your home? Your people?"

"Rainer fights his own battles. My home is now far away. My people are those near. Those I love, my brother and sister—and you." She paused, her declaration done. "And what of your home? Your mother? Your people?"

Shock blanched his handsome face.

She asked him to give up what was so rightfully his. An ancient lineage. A grand estate. Tenants who respected him. And his mother? Would that lady come if he bade her?

All that must have swirled through his mind, too, because he looked ravaged. But the storm in his thinking passed as his fingers dug into her shoulders.

"*Liesel.*" Her name on his lips was a dirge, and she knew he was refusing her.

She stepped backward out of his arms. She had failed. "I bid you adieu, sir."

"I forbid you to leave here."

She cast him a look filled with sweet goodbyes. "I say the same to you."

"I must."

She ached for the loss of him. "Where do you think you can go where the memory of me will not throb inside your very bones? What good work will you ever accomplish without me?"

She stepped back, away from temptation. She saw his reasons. Here in his home, she saw the fullness of it. Saw what he valued and what he sought to save. To leave it all, to end his fight against the French, would be a defeat for him.

She loved him too much to repeat her offer.

✦ ❧ ✦

Chapter Sixteen

"THANK YOU, MARY," Liesel said, dismissing the young maid. "I will ring for you in the morning when I need you."

She listened as the girl made her way to the sitting room beyond and close the door to the hall, then paced before her four-poster bed. The night was still young. She should be tired. Arriving at Fournier Park had been a relief. Dinner had been pleasant. Her bath, a long soak in the large tub, had been restful, restorative.

But her mind swam in sorrow.

Dirk would leave tomorrow, and she would never see him again. That would be the end of them, an abrupt abyss along the journey that had taken them over the hills and dales of hundreds of miles, leagues of sea—and stirring emotions full of conflict and the most tender craving.

She put a hand to her brow. She would not shed a tear over his departure. He had told her he would go, and she had argued as best she could.

But now she had only one need. One desire.

And she would show him that when he left, he took a part of her with him.

She padded into her sitting room and listened for anyone

walking the hall. She opened the door. No one was about.

A hand to the neckline of her robe, borrowed from his mother's trunks, as were the sheer muslin night rail and her slippers, she pulled open the door and peered out. The hall was clear.

Liesel had asked Mary about the layout of the house so she knew where she was going.

So reminiscent of that first time she had entered his life, she came into his suite and heard him dismissing his servant. The splash of water made her smile at the coincidence. He was again in his bath. All the better to waylay him.

She waited until she heard no more footsteps, his valet having retreated through his access at the back of the boudoir and into the servants' closets. Standing taller, she found the gumption she needed—and a smile.

She strolled in. He reclined in his bath, facing her. Naked amid floating soap bubbles, he sat looking like a dashing Bacchus, sleek skin, muscular torso, eyes flashing at her with surprise and humor.

Merry that he was not angry at her, she walked right up to him. Then she picked up his towel from his nearby stool and sat down.

He made no effort to cover himself. It wasn't necessary. She could see the important parts, most of all how he set his jaw, how his biceps flexed—and how his manhood rose.

His long, elegant fingers gripped the edge of his porcelain tub. "You make a habit of intruding on a man during his bath."

"I know. I do like it, and I promise not to change. I also like the fragrance of roses you've added to your bathwater."

He feigned disgruntlement. "It seems at the moment that is the only one they have in this house."

"I know," she said with a grin as she crossed one long, bare leg over the other and lifted an arm to her nose to inhale. "It's what I too was offered."

His gaze went limpid as it flowed over her hair and lips, her shoulders, down that bare leg to her toes. Dressed as she was in his mother's finest Dacca muslin nightgown, she knew that beneath the robe, which she had left untied, she appeared nearly nude to him.

"I like you best in lemon verbena."

His admission spiked her need of him. When he looked at her, so bedazzled, she had no way to hide her own enchantment. "I will take you any way at all."

He sucked in air. "Turn around."

She stared at him.

"So be it," he said beneath his breath, and in the next instant, he put those powerful hands to the porcelain and rose like a wild, disheveled god from the sea.

She watched him rise, his sinewy thighs, his lean hips, his long, hard, red penis. All that she wanted, and more, much more of him.

"Hand me the towel."

She did his bidding. She had not come to be a hellion.

He took it from her and dried himself off. Then, hooking the towel around his waist as he had done that first night she attacked him, he climbed out of his bath and padded to snatch up pants that sat folded upon another stool. She watched him climb into them and tie the ribbons at the waist. The pants fit loosely, cuffed at his ankles, an exotic flow of ruby Indian silk pajamas that teased her senses.

She wanted them off him, his leg pinning her to him, his skin hot on hers. But she swallowed. The time was not yet ripe, nor the place, so she strode away into his bedroom. He followed her.

Here were the elements that had defined his early life. A high chest of rich rosewood with silver pulls. A credenza of the same wood, his brush and comb placed just so. A few small bottles. A wall of shelves filled with books, old, newer, some well thumbed.

"You read *Pamela*?" She wished to spend her life discovering new aspects of his character.

"Doesn't everyone like a good romp?"

She waggled her brows at him. "I hope so."

He gave a short laugh. "Ah, yes. The wrong thing to say, eh?"

She wandered to his desk. It was a useful piece, japanned in black lacquer, a complement to the rosewood. Atop the desk lay a few sheets of paper, indicating how he had spent much of the afternoon at his letter writing.

"Will you see your friends in London?" She was jealous of them, having his company when she would be robbed of it.

He frowned. "If I have time."

"Why would you not make time?"

"*Liesel.*" He shook his head. His word was a weary warning to her not to proceed.

Too bad. She was here. Her time was now.

"Why would you not?" She dug in. "You control the agenda. No one knows you are in town."

"Visiting," he said as he strode to his liquor console and unstoppered a carafe, "is for those who are free. I am not. Never have been." He poured two glasses of some dark, rich liquid and returned to place one in her hand. "I will see Scarlett Hawthorne and her man of accounts, a huge, surly fellow who runs her records and helps her track of all their agents." He took a good swallow of his drink and marched to the window overlooking the gardens. "What else do you want to know?"

"Will you see your mother?"

She admired him in stark silhouette. His expression softened as he regarded her, his hazel eyes mellow with his love for the lady who had birthed and raised him. "I asked if she might meet me in London. She would never forgive me if I failed to honor her with a few minutes before I leave."

"More like you would not forgive yourself," Liesel added, and strolled to stand before him. There, in the dim candlelight from the sconces, she smiled. "I'd go with you to London, but you would not allow it."

He narrowed his gaze at her. "You are going to London and doing your own good work."

"I will. Day after tomorrow, I think. I stay only to ensure

Nikky and Katrin are happy and settling in here." She drained her glass.

He went to sit in the huge wing chair near the fire. "I will instruct Jameson to give you all that you need for your journey and more. If you need anything—money, carriage, clothes, a house—you must know I will give it all to you."

She huffed. She thought she had settled this. She had some money Becker had given her before they left Rittenburg. She hoped to have a goodly amount left in her accounts from years ago. Clothes she would acquire from her own townhouse when she arrived in London. To that city, she'd wear the gown and cloak she'd chosen from Dirk's mother's wardrobe. She'd take his coach, yes. Then send it back here.

She whirled to face him. Now she would tell him what she really needed. Her robe swung wide in the move, and the heavy brocade slid down one shoulder. The muslin gave away all that she was. And she would not move. Modesty would not contribute to her ambition.

So he looked. He savored and stared. From her eyes to her hair, to her breasts, her hips and her toes, he absorbed her. As his gaze wended back up, he did not breathe when he encountered the froth of hair at the juncture of her thighs, or how her nipples beaded high and hard against the transparent muslin. His fingers turned white as he gripped his glass. She marveled that he did not break it.

Then she went to him, putting her glass to the table beside him. Prying his glass from him to the table, too. She knelt before him and placed her hands on his thighs. Beneath the sinuous silk, she detected every arch, every plane of him that would be hers. She slid her hands up to his hips and raised her face to stare him in the eyes. "There is one thing you have not given me."

He exhaled and sank one hand in the wealth of her hair. His fingernails against her scalp, he said, "My darling woman, you know that is not wise."

She tipped her head into the caress of his hand. "Wisdom is

not useful here."

"It should be."

"You argue with me, but why?" She slid up over his lap and spread her fingers against the rock-hard power of his chest.

"I keep my word."

She moved so close that her lips were a whisper from his. "'Twas you who vowed you would not kiss me again."

He curled his fingers in her hair. His gaze grew pained—and she knew not if it was with hope or defeat.

Her heart broke that she tortured him so. "But I did not promise I would not kiss you."

"You should, sweetheart," he whispered. "You should."

But then his voice drifted away as her lips were on his, and all words—all vows, all promises—dissolved in the delirium of the now.

⊱⊱⊰⊰

He tore his lips from hers. "I swore I would not do this, Liesel."

"This is my decision. My need."

His lips opened. No sound came forth.

"Deny me," she challenged him.

His torment melted away, until all that was left of him was his undying desire for her.

She slid forward, and her mouth was on his, her heart atop his—and he would take her and offer her the world for one brief ecstasy.

So then she kissed him. Kissed him with all the longing of the past weeks. All the sorrow and terror and desire they'd endured. All the successes they had gained.

He cupped her cheeks and drew her lips to his again. She was soft and sweet, and he needed every bit of her. Her lips, her tongue, her teeth. How was it possible that he could not get enough of her?

He pulled her up over him, his mouth devouring hers. This was bliss he'd not known. Not anticipated. How could he have not enjoyed her, reveled in her, before now?

He sat forward, his mouth taking and giving. Then he pushed her away and heaved himself up. He took her with him, then swept her high into his arms.

She made a little sound that told him she was alarmed he'd leave her.

"I'm not going anywhere, my darling. You've come to me. Claimed me." He kissed her. "Commanded me. And by God, you'll have me."

He strode to his bed and set her down on the edge. Brushing her robe away, he smoothed the muslin gown down her shoulders and over the globes of her breasts. Her large, pretty pink nipples stood, pointed and eager for his caresses. He sucked in his breath, bent, lifted one round, firm sphere, and laved and nipped her. She was made for him. He'd known at first glance that he was hers by rights of heaven and earth.

Her hands at his shoulders, he did homage to her other breast. But even that was not enough. He found the hem of her gown and the long, elegant curves of her calves and thighs.

In a rush of madness, he tore the gown from her, up and over her head.

The corners of her mouth turned slowly up in approval. She was not embarrassed. Not his Liesel. She was giving him all he wished.

He stared down at her beauty. His imagination had been so frail. Here beneath his fingers was the smooth line of her collarbone, the dip between her heavy breasts, her large, round nipples, her waist so small, her hips so wide, and her thighs open to his reach.

He dropped his head to her shoulder. He needed strength, resolve that he would go slowly. That he'd make this so sweet, so delicious for her that she would not, *could* not, hate him in the years to come.

He put a hand to her shoulder and pushed her back to the bed. With a look of an angel possessed, she went down and reached for him.

He pushed her slender thighs wider. Her allowing him so near, given her horrid past, told him that she trusted him. Yes, she loved him.

He dropped a kiss to the crevice between her thigh and her heavy folds.

She arched up in supplication for more of that, and he caught fast breaths, eager to lick and taste and savor all she was.

With a gentle hand smoothing her hip, he cupped her heavy lips and nudged her open for him. She complied, one of her legs up over his back.

The fragrance of roses melded with the musk of her arousal. He moaned, overcome. With gentle fingers, he spread her wide and dipped his tongue inside her.

She bucked, but he soothed her. And then he took more of her.

He sank one finger into her slick, hot channel and, with his thumb, found her clitoris. He polished the little nub, and sent her lolling her head upon the covers.

She gasped his name, and he gave her more.

Still, none of it was enough. He was ravenous. He'd expected this, told her that once he had made love to her, he'd never stop, never waver, never relent until he owned every part of her.

He rose, pushed down his pajamas, and threw them to the bed. Then he crawled up over her, his elbows to the mattress, smiling down at her and whispering how he would ensure this would erase all she'd known before with a careless man.

"You ensured that weeks ago, my darling," she murmured, and caught his mouth in a demanding kiss.

He brushed tendrils of hair from her cheek. Tears scalded his eyes and joy filled his heart. "I love you."

His words transformed her lovely face into a beatific look of grace. "I know. I know."

He kissed his way down her ribs to her stomach and her hipbone. Then he took himself in hand and slid his length along her wet flesh. He set his teeth at the thrill of her heat and the spike of his voracious need.

He spread her lips wider and, bit by bit, sank in deep and deeper.

She held her breath, her eyes wide upon him. "More," she pleaded, and sank her nails into his biceps.

Her invitation gave him courage, but her past experience, brutal as it was, made him careful. He kissed her throat, the top of her breast, and sought inside himself all the tenderness he bore her. If he was to make love to her—and so far into the act, he would not stop now—he would treasure each part of her. He'd show her by his every sigh that he valued all she was. He'd never hurt her. Never disappoint her. Not on his life.

His life.

He pulled away and admired all of her bare to him. He swept a hand down her elegant torso. Her body was his. His life was hers, had been since that second time she'd come to him and needed his help. His heart was hers, too, since every waking moment, and every one asleep, had been spent rejoicing in who and what she was. No woman had ever struck him with her beauty as she had. No woman had ever held him with her character as she had.

He smiled at her. "I have not told you enough how I love you."

Her lips spread wide in a grin. "Tell me as often as you wish. I will never tire of the words."

The dam holding back his wildest desires broke. "I want to be your man."

"You are! You have been from the very night I asked for help."

"I want to be the man who is worthy of you, a man of good repute. A man respected by his peers. I want to change what I am perceived to be so that I can be all you should have as your husband."

"You can change the past. You can find a way."

He kissed her deeply. "I must imbibe your faith in me."

She undulated against him, her gaze afire with her need. "Then come inside me, please, and take all of me. I gladly give you all I have." Her words were a plea for the rest of the act, her fingers digging into his arms, kneading, demanding all he could give her.

He began to move slowly, cautious to bring her along with him. She smiled at him and urged him down to kiss her.

He lowered his head to taste her earlobe and throat. She was everything he had dreamed of, hot and giving and liquid in his arms. He urged her higher, brought her legs up over his thighs so that he could reach more of her, take all of her. All at once, he was in, high to her hilt, full to his length.

With a few exquisite moves, he lost his mind to the rhythm that consumed them. In her slick warmth, she came, pulsing and sighing.

He marveled at her quick surrender to desire. He marveled at his own.

He was a man possessed by her. So when he reached the point where he had to have her with him, he also marveled that she arched and bucked and throbbed. But, careful not to spoil her more, he yanked away, caught himself, and spilled into his discarded pajamas.

She moaned in objection and rolled toward him. But he had done what he must.

He would not harm her more and chance a child.

He took her into his embrace and held her tightly. His lips in her hair, he rubbed her back while she kissed his throat and made him think of how this union should last forever.

SHE AWOKE TO the movement of the mattress. He had made love to her a second time and, like after the first, held her close afterward. Now, cool air replaced the warm haven of his arms as he left the bed.

Naked, he strode away. A few candles still burned low and played in myriad shadows across his carved physique.

That second time he had loved her, he'd shown her more of a poignant declaration of love. He'd taken his time to show her how passion could rise and fall and rise again. He'd kissed each inch of her, turning her to her back, tasting the skin of her waist and her thigh, her calf, and even her big toe. He'd spread wide her thighs to find and tease and polish some small space between her folds that drove her, panting, to some blind heaven filled with rosy bliss. Silently, he had entered her again and taken her with him to a stunning climax where they both held, suspended in a euphoria she would recall to her last breath.

She watched him now. Detached, he wore that fixed expression when he debated an issue with himself. He poured water from a glass pitcher into two small glasses. The delicate sound of splashes made her smile.

When he returned, he sat beside her and bent to kiss her.

"Drink," he said as he handed her a glass.

The water was cool, refreshing.

"How do you feel?" He threaded his fingers into her hair.

"Never more alive."

He gave a laugh. "Good." But then, frowning, he pushed away.

"Come back," she urged him.

"This cannot be a habit."

"You're leaving," she said with concern and mounting anger. Then she abruptly sat up. "How can it become a habit?"

He set his jaw, his brilliant eyes ablaze. "Because now I have a taste of you, I want all of you!"

There was the sum of their challenge. She swung her legs over the edge of the bed. "All or nothing."

"If I try—" He stared at her, his hope mingling with his frustration in the shake of his head. "I cannot promise a thing."

At least she had brought him that far—and there, on the edge of that abyss, she would meet him. She picked up her gown and robe, then clutched them to her naked body. "Nor I."

But she had acquired here what she needed for herself. She hoped she'd given him fond memories, too, if, in their years ahead, they had only this night to sustain them.

"Never forget me." His voice was a wreck.

So many had forgotten him, used him, ignored him. She absorbed the strength and power and despair of him, virile, tormented creature that he was. She loved him with every bone, muscle, vein in her body. "I remember your every smile, every word, every valiant act. Until we meet again, my darling, know that you live in me, as I live in you."

Then, having given him everything, she left him where he stood.

Chapter Seventeen

St. Katherine's Dock
London
June 4, 1804

SCARLETT HAWTHORNE GREETED Dirk, arms wide to embrace him. "We were very concerned about you, Fournier."

"Your runner out of Karlsruhe," said Todd Carlton, her man of all work, "sent word you had left, but for ten weeks, we've had nothing."

Dirk had taken a room in a coaching inn on the South Bank last night. There, as in the hours of his journey north, all he thought of was the possible means by which he could save his reputation, save his future, and save his need to have the Crown Princess of Rittenburg as his own.

He would not go to Fournier House to alert his staff or others he was in Town. To meet his chief agent and her assistant Carlton, he had hired an innkeeper's son to run to Scarlett's office in the City and ask her to meet him in one of her secret houses.

This one was in St. Katherine's Dock near London Bridge. From the outside, the pile appeared to be a tumbledown half-timbered cottage, a remnant from Tudor times. The interior was fit out with every comfortable and useful amenity. A full pantry, clean linens, even a change of clothes, men's, women's, and children's. All of it was for those agents who needed shelter, rest, or sanctuary for a night or more.

"Please, let us sit." Scarlett took a chair, folding her long fingers over the plain gown she'd worn as disguise to come here. She was a beautiful woman with dark auburn hair and deep green eyes, usually very well dressed—but here in the docks, she was right to wear no such finery. "Tell us the details of your journey."

Dirk ran through a summary of his sojourn from Karlsruhe to Kent. He included Prince Rainer's appearance in Koblenz and the rumors of the French army assembling on the coast of the Channel. By Scarlett's nod, she knew of the army's movements, but not of Rainer's. Dirk concluded by telling them, "Everyone is healthy."

"And the princess?" Carlton stood to one side of Scarlett, his hands behind his back.

What to tell them? That he loved her? That he had to find a way to keep her? That he had few clues how that could be achieved? He was grasping at wisps of air with only hope to lead him on. "She is recovering well at Fournier Park but leaving to come here to London soon. She wants her brother and sister to adjust well to their new surroundings."

"And you?" Scarlett asked in a light tone that elicited a smile from him.

"I am well."

"But...?"

She detected every nuance of a person's state of mind. It was why she'd succeeded at running a spy ring so successful that even prime ministers envied her results.

He would be bold. "But I fear I have outlived my usefulness."

"Not entirely, sir," Carlton interjected. "We doubt you can return to the Continent. Too many know your face."

"Indeed." Scarlett smoothed her skirt of pale green cotton. "As soon as Princess Elizabeth reports to the queen, everyone will know your deeds."

Dirk flinched. "I would hope for discretion, but I doubt anyone within earshot of Liesel's story will refrain from telling it."

Scarlett's brows rose at his reference to Elizabeth by her diminutive.

"The *ton* will embroider it, too," Carlton added—and by his sour tone, was none too pleased by it.

"What do you *want* to do, Fournier?" Scarlett asked. "You have earned the right to name it."

"Ah, well." Dirk had hoped for that, but there was only so much his friends could do against the influence of the court and Society. "What I want and what I need are two different things."

"Are they? Let us examine that. Pour us each a good whisky, Carlton." Scarlett stared at Dirk as her man strode away to do her bidding. "You have been away from us for more than two years, dear sir. You have missed much. Your best friends—Ashley, Ramsey, and Appleby—all are home, safe, healthy, and prospering. They and their wives work for us here to great benefit. I would think with your skills, you too would find fulfillment in a slightly more intricate espionage at home."

"I would welcome that." *If I were a man made whole, I could more easily find a way to have Liesel for my own.*

"But you need a little help from us. Doesn't he, Carlton?"

The man nodded in agreement.

Scarlett considered Dirk with soft compassion. "I am happy to tell you of a few things that may help you. A few things that have happened lately that may color your opinion of staying in Britain."

"That I am eager to hear."

"I am informed by our agent in Manchester that Alice Sedgwick has had a change of circumstances."

Dirk sighed. "She could go to hell and I could not care to hear about it."

"But she is *in* hell." Scarlett locked her forest-green eyes on Dirk's. "Three weeks ago, she lost her child to the ague."

Dirk felt the blow, remembering his own mother's grief at the loss of his two young brothers. "That must be difficult."

"In the midst of her mourning, however, she has found some

relief."

He looked away and back again. "I cannot begrudge her that."

"Nor can Carlton and I deprive you of this relief: Oliver, Lord Fellowes, married her last week."

Fellowes had been the one who'd kissed her and had her at that house party. Dirk had been the one to discover them in *flagrante delicto* in the garden. Then others at the party had discovered him talking with Alice, trying to console her, soon after Fellowes fled the scene. Knowing the wrath of her parents and Fellowes's father, the two had blamed the seduction on Dirk. Fellowes was a bully and a braggart and had always disliked Dirk. He had told Alice's brother that Dirk raped Alice. But it was plot to blackmail Dirk and make him pay a ransom to him. Dirk had refused. He'd fought the duel instead against her brother, won, then left the country. Alice and Fellowes had been foiled, their scheme ruined. But also in the process, Alice had been shamed. Fellowes had been forced by his father to marry a wealthy merchant's daughter, and was then cut off financially by his father. Alice, Fellowes, and his new, innocent young wife had all been ruined.

"I knew Fellowes's wife," Scarlett said with pity. "She was always very sickly. Poor girl was sweet and kind and did not deserve the life she was forced to live. She died three months ago."

"Fellowes hurried to Manchester," Carlton added as he came toward Dirk with whiskies, "when he heard of his child's death."

Dirk sighed. "I am glad to hear he had the decency to marry Alice."

Carlton said, "It removes some of the taint against you."

"But not all." Scarlett took her own glass from Carlton and drank.

"No." Dirk scoffed. "Not Fellowes's threat to kill me."

Carlton placed a glass in his hand. "Not that. But there are other means."

"I am here to learn them, Carlton."

"Would you consider remaining in England?"

"I would." Dirk took a healthy swallow of his drink. "Do you have a magic wand that exonerates me of my failures?"

"But they are not failures, are they?" Carlton pressed him.

"They are enough to ban me from full Society."

"How important to you is a return to the *ton*?" Scarlett asked.

Dirk dropped all politesse and stared at his superior. "If I had my wish, I would return home to cultivate my fields and tend to my tenants. I would..." He paused to imagine Liesel dancing in his arms, laughing naked in his bed, all his. "I would find a way to be the gentleman my father raised me to be. I would rid everyone's mind of the Alice and Fellowes scandal and allow some to know what service I have done for the Crown. I would work for you here."

An appreciative smile spread on Scarlett's pretty lips. "Have you a method to achieve any of that?"

He barked with laughter. His hopes were mere fantasies that had blossomed for him after Liesel had come to him and loved him so well in his bed. "I have thought of one. I hope you might help me with that."

"Good man." Carlton downed his whisky. "Name it."

Dirk's mind was suddenly full of whimsy—and hope. "You are acquainted, I do believe, with a man in Seven Dials by the name of Dáire O'Neill?"

Carlton came around to sit in a chair opposite Dirk. His meaty hands clasped together, he bent toward Dirk. "Our fixer?"

Dirk nodded. The Irishman ran a gambling hell in the poorest part of London. Known to the public as a criminal, O'Neill in reality kept a clean house. No prostitutes, no smuggling, no dens of opium. Yet he knew who ran them. And his livelihood was in arranging the correction of innocent people's false condemnations.

"Fancy a favor from him?" Scarlett had a merry twinkle in her dark eyes.

Dirk sat back, relief washing through him. "I wonder if O'Neill holds any markers of Fellowes's."

She beamed. "I think you must ask him."

DÁIRE O'NEILL, SO said those who dared to describe him, was as invisible as the legendary giants who had once walked the green valleys of Ireland. Most in Britain had never seen him. But to be shown to his presence was not an experience one soon forgot.

Towering over most men, built like an ox with hands that could span a man's throat, fast as the gangly gray wolfhounds he kept at his side, Dáire could also be a man or woman's best friend...or their deadly enemy. He'd gained a reputation in Dublin during the rebellion of '98 as a fierce fighter. Discouraged by the rebels' failure, he decided to move to London to learn about the conqueror up close. He'd earned his prowess boxing, his fortune betting against wild odds, and his fame righting wrongs done by powerful fools over lesser ones. In the past four years as one of the two most powerful men in London's underworld, he'd possessed money, influence, and knowledge that those in Whitehall and Carlton House envied—and often cultivated.

He ran his kingdom of cardsharps and informers as tightly as a Royal Navy captain ran his sailors, renowned for his refusal to run brothels and employ children. Many questioned how Dáire excelled. "A right cove" was not a phrase he favored, but in his dealings with friend or foe, he demanded ethics. He had rules of engagement for those jobs he took. Those who worked for him had laws to live by. To break them meant one did not enjoy his favor again. Ever. Because he never forgot a violation. Never forgave an error. Never countenanced a foe.

Dáire knew well who his friends were. He kept lists of those in government who played fairly, and another list of those who did not. He had one archenemy, his rival, Jonathan Rivers. Below that, so said those who dealt with Dáire, were those who cheated at horses or cards, abused others by word or deed. If one had a grievance against another, proof of the crime was required first. Then compensation to Dáire, as well as to the victims, had better be extraordinary.

Dirk went alone into the hell that was Seven Dials. Carlton had requested an appointment and safe passage through the gray-black hell that comprised the crumbling buildings of the rookery. How Dirk was known among those who tracked his entry to the slums, he had no idea.

Carlton had given him directions and advice: "Straight through the main courtyard. Try not to appear too alarmed by those with a knife or a pistol at the ready."

Dirk knocked upon the broad oak door, the forest-green paint peeling. One of O'Neill's body men opened the screeching door. He curled his lip, surly as one needed to be to survive in the underbelly of London's back streets.

"Fournier? Aye, Mister O'Neill said you can come." He pulled the door wider.

Dirk stood in a foyer so bright with polished marble that he had to blink.

"Up!" Another brute of a guard appeared and ran his hands over every inch of his body. For that rude groping, Dirk was granted a grunt and a nod toward the richly red-carpeted stairs. "Follow me."

At the top of the stairs, his escort knocked twice upon the door. When it was opened by a troll three feet tall, the little man barked out Dirk's name and led him forward.

Two gray wolfhounds bounded forward, as tall as his chest. He stood quite still and let them smell him. He'd humor them, otherwise he might not live beyond the next minute.

"Bring him in, O'Malley," a rough bass voice said from the room at the end of the hall. "The dogs'll follow."

Dirk rounded the threshold to come face to face with the

smiling visage of a burly black Irishman with wild curls, a deep sea tan, and the fine tailoring that usually denoted a gentleman of the *ton*.

"Good to have you, Lord Fournier. Please do come in. Finn, you may leave us. And take the boys with you, will you please? That's a lad. Whisky, sir?" O'Neill indicated one of the big, polished wooden chairs before his desk.

"Aye, I understand one does not drink anything but good Irish spirits between these walls."

"Good man. John Power & Son it is." O'Neill took his time pouring into tall crystal glasses. "They're my ma's cousins. One has to patronize the family, you see."

"Keep them hail and hearty. Yes." Dirk raised his glass in a toast. "I know that rule well."

"I have confirmation you do, sir. Saved more than twenty of your family and relatives from the scourge of the little Frenchman."

Whether O'Neill had learned that recently from Carlton and Scarlett or knew it from his own sources, Dirk was happy to have his bona fides established before they talked business.

"Thank you," Dirk said, and sipped. "Good spirits."

"Helps whet a man's appetite for a fine meal." O'Neill took the chair behind his broad mahogany desk. "I understand you have a certain type of cuisine in mind."

"I do. I might at one time have called it revenge, but what I truly seek now is something more rewarding."

"Name it."

"Restoration."

O'Neill raised his own glass brimming with amber liquid. "You need it done to this scoundrel Fellowes."

"I do."

"He once ruined everything he touched. Women, his father's finances, his sister's prospects for a good marriage, Alice Sedgwick."

"And me."

"And you. Yes, I know the story well. I have a book, you see, with such details, lest I forget a detail or two." O'Neill tipped his head toward the circular library table that stood in the center of the room.

"Your bible, is it?" Dirk appreciated this man more each minute.

"In my work, one must have facts. Names, dates. The truth always slays best."

"Scarlett Hawthorne and Todd Carlton have led me to believe you may know facts about Fellowes that may free me once and for all of his slurs upon my name and character. I am most eager to remain here in my home and continue to work for the Crown. I am prepared to compensate you any fee if you might help me do that."

"It so happens that the man has invested his deceased wife's inheritance into a holding company of African-Caribbean slavers."

Dirk felt lightheaded. Few commercial prospects were worse than selling human beings. "A new venture, is it?"

"Exactly," O'Neill said with a grimace. "He has sunk his money into this holding company with three of his friends, none of whom I would allow to wipe the dirt from my boots."

Dirk sat forward. "Slavers earn rich profits. Ten to twenty times the initial investment."

"Oh, that's true." O'Neill waved his glass around. "If all four of them were only a bit smarter and investigated where their money actually had gone, which was to my bank account, they might not have had this problem. But they did not. It is quite sad that they will all soon find themselves in debtor's prison."

"How might that help me get Fellows to absolve me publicly of all blame in Alice's seduction?"

O'Neill smacked his lips. "I think I might offer Fellowes a chance to take half his money out before the truth about his hollow corporation is printed in the papers."

"I see." Dirk grinned. "Half his money is better than none."

"Half is sizable—generous, even. But a reprobate never does

get complete reward of all his wealth. That leaves a man with nothing to aspire to, don't you think?"

Fellowes would have some means to live out his life with Alice. Perhaps in their own sordid way, they cared for each other and could make a good life together. "About how much is half of his current wealth?"

"Ten thousand."

"So. Not a fortune."

"But more than he'll have if he does not issue public apologies to you."

"This seems too easy."

"It will be. You catch a man by grabbing him in his own vice. Greed has been one of his."

Lust and envy the other two. "Mr. O'Neill, I would be delighted to pay your fee for such a magnificent service."

"Fee? No. No, you owe me none."

"But for such a good deed, one must always see a significant reward."

"Oh, I do gain one, Fournier. Never doubt. You see, I may serve notice to Lord Fellowes that he must dissolve his share of the slavers, but I will not grant such a favor to his three friends."

"I see. And if those three each have a total investment of twenty thousand in this fake company, then when you dissolve it, you come into sixty thousand pounds. Plus ten of Fellowes's money. A handsome amount."

"A job well done."

"Slavers destroyed. Ten thousand to live on to Fellowes and Alice."

"Restitution for you, Fournier." O'Neill pushed back his chair as he rose. Then he put out his hand.

But Dirk felt off kilter. As if he were aboard Jacques Durand's sloop, he seemed to have lost his balance or his compass. "I wonder, do you have the address for Fellowes in Manchester?"

DIRK LEFT O'NEILL'S minutes later and walked toward the Thames. He hailed a hack, climbed in, and dug out his pocket watch. He had ten minutes to make it to Gunter's. Buoyed by his success with O'Neill and his hope to be useful to Scarlett here at home, he had one more request of another person.

His mama would never refuse him. He smiled, especially if he told her she could expect to see him regularly—daily, if she wished. And with a wife beside him, too.

Chapter Eighteen

No. 20 Hanover Square
London
June 6, 1804

LIESEL CRUSHED THE morning newspaper as she sat at her breakfast table and muttered a few blue words none of her servants should hear. She had completely forgotten that June fifth was His Majesty's birthday. All of London had lined the route from the Queen's House at Buckingham yesterday morning down to St. James's Palace. The festivities, abridged for the health and welfare of the sixty-six-year-old monarch, had gone on, nonetheless, for more than six hours. The weather had not cooperated. Not outside the palace, nor inside, where closed windows and doors made the air so close in such a crush of celebrants that several ladies had fainted and were carried out. *Lifeless,* declared one newspaper.

In spite of it all, the ceremony went on, with Her Majesty receiving the nobility, the gentry, and the diplomatic corps. Musical selections by Handel were ordered up, and only after six o'clock did the royal family retire to the Queen's House once more.

Liesel would not expect anyone to even entertain the idea of having an audience with the queen today. Perhaps not tomorrow, either. They were all exhausted from the folderol. There had even been some sort of conflict between military guards and local police. A few men were wounded and the queen had been notified, to her distress.

All of which meant Liesel would be wise to do her other business today. She'd go to the bank and see if Becker had managed to get Rothschild to transfer her allowance. Afterward, if she had a mind for some more frivolous activity, she'd call on her modiste. Liesel had tried on a few of her gowns hanging in her wardrobe upstairs, and contrary to her hopes, they did not fit her well. She was thinner from her recent travels, yet with her age, she was also more buxom. Nor were her clothes the latest in fashion. She might not have worn the most stylish garb for the past few years, but she knew when a gown was too old or tired to wear to face the queen.

Two hours later, she took the stairs down to her foyer. Pulling on her gloves, she encountered her butler.

Selfless soul that he was, he asked if she wished him to notify Cook of anything special she'd like for her dinner. "We three do not keep a large pantry, Your Highness."

"I understand, Mr. Martin. Nothing special for me, thank you, and do thank Cook. Whatever all of you were going to have, I will too."

"Have you any expectation of how long you remain with us, Your Highness?"

"Not yet, Martin. Perhaps tomorrow or the next day."

"Very well, ma'am. I will go hail a carriage for you."

LIESEL WATCHED CLIVE Davenport, Marquess of Carlisle, as he hurried along Upper Brook Street. He walked from his house in Grosvenor Square to his sister's in Park Street every day at four. Today was no exception.

His hand on his hat, his head down against the patter of rain, he approached her.

She stood upon the corner, her parasol up, hoping it might withstand any sudden downpour.

"My lord," she greeted him with a smile as he came closer.

He paused a moment to blink at the sight of her. Then he grinned. "My dear woman." He scanned the street to see who might observe them, then took her arm, as had been their custom in years gone by when she would come to report to him. They would pretend to promenade, as if they were friends, which they had over the years become. "How good of you to come see me. When, by God's grace, did you arrive in London?"

"Only last night."

He slowed his pace to gaze upon her and take in details. "You look well."

"Hmm, do I?" She gave him a wistful toss of her head. She was as well dressed as she could be. Felt as well as could be. "You certainly are a man of discretion. I know I am not fit at the moment to be walking far. My sea legs are still with me. The crossing from Bremen to Yarmouth was so chaotic, I may bob up and down for years."

"A frightful route." He chuckled. "But, Your Highness," he whispered, "I am so glad to see you."

He was a charming man, a politician, a diplomat, and a master of spies. Taller than she by a few inches, with sun-bleached brown hair and long-lashed gray eyes, he was by her guess in his mid-thirties. A widower, he was also a father of a little girl. The child who was so young when she lost her mother needed a nurturing woman in her life...and Carlisle's older sister had become that for the girl. He took her there each morning at eight and fetched her each afternoon at four. If ever Liesel had children, she would hope her husband would bless their offspring with as much love as this man did his.

But that was a fantasy. Only Dirk Fournier would do for her, and he was as much a black sheep as she. Never would they be restored to their own rightful places, let alone to a normal place in this rigid Society.

She caught her breath. Today marriage and children seemed so impossible to her.

Carlisle paused upon the paved street. They stood before his sister's house. "Shall we go in to talk?"

The two of them had met there before. Liesel would call upon Terese, Lady Winterton, and that lady would send a note to Carlisle of Liesel's need to speak with him. Carlisle would arrive soon after, often by the kitchen door for secrecy's sake.

"Yes, let's."

Carlisle led them up the steps and tapped with the knocker. The butler appeared in a trice. Recognizing Liesel as the one who'd often met his mistress's brother in secret, he ushered them both in to the small family parlor at the back of the first-floor stairs.

"Give us ten minutes, Brown," Carlisle instructed the butler. "I know my sister will wish to greet our visitor. But we need some time alone."

"Certainly, sir." Brown bowed himself away.

Carlisle patted her hand as she took a chair before the fireplace. A small fire burned, chasing away the chill of the rain.

"I am quite thrilled to see you, Liesel."

"I am quite thrilled to be here, Clive."

"Conditions are so grave on the Continent, we worried you were captured."

She would summarize her plight as best she could. Details she would give to Carlisle and his three colleagues later. "You were right to be concerned. I was there, Clive, when Caulaincourt came across the Rhine to capture the Duke of Enghien. I saw the army arrive at his house. I know I could do nothing to save him, but God knows I tried. And I fled."

"Where did you go? I had no word, no clue from any of our assets in Germany or France."

"I went to Lord Fournier."

"In Karlsruhe?" That shocked him. "Do you know some say

he works for Scarlett Hawthorne?"

"I have heard that rumor, yes." She gave him a rueful look. She would not reveal information that only Dirk could utter. "I knew how he'd saved so many these past two years, and with the abduction of Enghien, I feared the French would invade more German states. Worse, I feared they'd abduct my sisters and brother for ransom."

"Liesel," he murmured in soft compassion, "we know Bonaparte did have a plan for that. He sent ten soldiers to Rittenburg."

She gasped. "When?"

"Early April. A secret operation that failed because you and your family were nowhere to be found."

"Thanks to Lord Fournier's quick thinking."

Carlisle leaned toward her. "And you are all safe?"

"My younger brother Nikky and my sister Katrin are here with me, safe and sound at Dirk's house in Kent."

Carlisle caught her informality. "Dirk?"

"Yes, I use his given name. One does not travel for weeks on end with anyone and not become their friend."

"At the very least."

At the most for me.

"But what of Mara?" he asked.

"She is married to Prince Hartenburg."

He went still with shock. "We've had no notice of that."

She frowned. "Have you no diplomatic announcement of their marriage?"

"None."

She put a hand to her throat. "Why would that be? They were married by the bishop in Rittenburg. I was there. So was Dirk. Hartenburg took Mara away that afternoon. Why is their marriage not public in his state?"

"I do not know. Perhaps any communiques from Hartenburg are delayed with the French crossing all sorts of boundaries and breaking rules. But I will inquire."

Her pulse pounded. She feared for her sister's welfare.

"Hartenburg wanted regent authority over Rittenburg. He thought he could get it, too, because when Dirk and I arrived, Rainer was not in residence and neither was I." She shot to her feet. "He is devious. You must ask the envoy from Hartenburg why they have no news of this marriage."

"I will. Never fear. Now, you must tell me what you did in Paris and how you managed to befriend Enghien. We need to know of your *success*, my dear."

She grinned. "I will gladly tell you all I learned. One thing I did was learn, painfully, was how to peel garlic in René Vaillancourt's kitchen."

"No!" Carlisle barked with laughter.

"I don't wish to do it again. Peel garlic, yes. Work for Vaillancourt, no. But I must add that I can now make a very good *pot-au-feu*, if you are interested."

"Ha! I will take you up on that. What else did you learn?"

"Vaillancourt is rabid for promotion. Evidently, he was very attached to one special lady, a friend of Josephine Bonaparte. But she deceived him, somehow. A friend carried her out of Vaillancourt's house in sight of many diplomats and military men. It was a scandal."

Carlisle seemed tickled by her explanation. "Madame St. Antoine is that lady. And yes, she was ill but carried away by the Englishman who loves here. She is now here in England and is Lady Ramsey. It is my understanding that she and her husband work for Scarlett Hawthorne. Ramsey has for years."

"Friends and spies are everywhere, aren't they?" She wondered if Dirk knew of this. Hopefully, here in Town, he would learn.

Carlisle agreed. "I wish more detail about your time abroad in coming days, please. But today, we speak of your future. First you must rest. Recover. Weeks of fright can tear at a person's health. I know. I remember."

Liesel recalled his wife's long illness, painful and debilitating, her malady robbing Carlisle of peace as he watched her slowly pass away.

"I wonder if you have any idea of what you would like to do from this day forward," he said.

She stared at him, this sweet man, this loving father, who coincidentally ran ruthless agents throughout Europe. "I want to leave London and go south to the sea. Brighton, I think. I want to make a good home for my brother and sister. That means I will not, for the immediate future, take any assignments from you."

"I understand. Know, however, I can arrange all that. What about funds? Do you need them?"

"I have money, thank you. What I do not have is pardon from Her Majesty for my behavior and a dissolution of my engagement contact with the Duke of Isenhurst. What service I have done for Crown and country should buy me both of those."

"I agree, Liesel. I will speak to the prime minister. He will know of your trials and tribulations—but most of all, your successes."

"I beg of you, Clive," she said as hot tears welled in her eyes, betraying her wish to appear strong, "set me free."

He took both her hands in his. "You deserve no less—and so much more."

LIESEL LEFT CARLISLE and his sister more than an hour later. The rain clouds had cleared. Did the heavens know the sun shone in her heart? Feeling gay, more than she had been in months, perhaps years, she decided to walk home.

She had much to tell Martin, her maid of all work, and Cook. They would applaud her future—or as much of it that she could predict at the moment. She wished she could tell Dirk about all her good news today. She had money from Becker. She had hope from Carlisle. Now all she needed was a fine gown, worthy of court, and the gumption to confront the queen to be removed from all her obligations to that woman's family. *Then* she would reveal all her good news to Dirk and pray that was enough to inspire him to free himself.

But where was he?

If he had returned to the Continent and not told her, she would be furious with him. In her worst moments in the middle of the night, when she missed his arms around her most, she would swear she would go after him. Although, as the sun rose, her better judgment told her that she could not leave Nikky and Katrin alone in this new world.

So where are you, Dirk? The nights are frightful without you.

She was on her second or third attempt to rid herself of her fears for him when she rounded the corner toward her house in the square.

A very fashionable lady was climbing down from her highly polished, ruby-lacquered town coach just in front of Liesel's house. She walked right up the front steps and knocked. When Martin opened the door, she announced herself and presented her card to the butler.

But Liesel needed no calling card to tell her who this lady was. From the moment she laid eyes on the woman's white-blonde hair and flashing brown eyes, she knew she would soon greet Baroness Fournier, Dirk's mother.

"Baroness, I am honored to meet you," Liesel said, inside. Martin had shown her guest into her parlor.

"*Danke schön,* Your Highness." The lady gave a flawless little bow. "As I am to meet you."

"I see my butler has done his duty to welcome you. My cook is very skilled, though lately, because I am so recently arrived, she has not as many delicacies as we would wish. But I will call for tea. Please"—she swept out a hand—"we will not stand on formality."

"No formality nor tea for me. Thank you, Your Highness." The woman folded her hands in her lap. She was a beauty, a mass of curls done up in the latest coif, and large doe eyes that faceted in shades of brown in the sunshine pouring though Liesel's window. "I am very happy to make your acquaintance. My son told me so much about you that I immediately became more eager to meet you."

"How kind of you." *And where is your son?* "I have had the same privilege of learning about you, my lady."

"Months escaping the wrath of Bonaparte gives you much time to reveal who you really are."

"It does."

"And what you want."

"That too." Liesel would not dilly-dally about this. "I want quite a lot."

"I know that too. And I came today to discuss that."

Memories of Dirk's mother flittered about in Liesel's head. She'd met her, perhaps once or twice, years ago. The lady had always been kind to her. But Liesel recalled too that the lady had waited on the queen with devotion. If this woman, who was one of the queen's ladies-in-waiting, had come here to discourage Liesel from breaking with the queen, she would be disappointed. If Dirk never got free of the stain on his character, if he never felt restored to his good name, Liesel did not care. She loved him no matter what the world thought of him. And if he returned, and if he still cared for her, she would do anything to live out her life with him.

But she grew uneasy. Odd as it was, Liesel wished for something in hand to fiddle. A cup. A biscuit. A scepter to command the situation. "I am happy to have you here, Lady Fournier. But if you come to discourage me from—"

"Forgive me," the baroness said with a kindly light in her brown eyes, "I come to you today because Dirk cannot."

"No?" Liesel watched, her heart in her hands, as Lady Fournier removed a letter from her reticule.

"Dirk has made his way to Manchester on a matter of personal business. He sends his loving regards." The lady leaned toward the low table between them and placed on it the small, sealed letter. "From Dirk to you, Your Highness."

Liesel bit her lower lip, restraining herself from snatching up the paper and devouring every word.

"He is quite restless without you."

That insight into his emotions, Liesel had not expected. But then, she was quite restless without him, too. "I hope he has the stamina to do what he must in Manchester."

"Do you know what he does, Your Highness?"

"No. Should I?"

"Our conversation was brief. I do not know all that has passed between the two of you."

That might be prudent. If he'd told his mother that they had been intimate, Liesel would die of embarrassment.

"Dirk is in the north, disentangling himself from the lies that were told about him years ago."

That had Liesel smiling. "Oh, I do wish him well in that. It will not be easy, whatever his plan is. But he so rightly deserves exoneration."

"Indeed he does. He is the finest man, full of spirit, and devotion to those he loves." Lady Fournier regarded Liesel with shrewd eyes. "He wishes to change his life."

"I wish him well."

"And would you join him if he succeeds?"

"I would say, ma'am, that the question really is, *could* I join him if he succeeds. And my answer is that I would if I were free."

"Freedom often has a price."

Liesel brought up her chin—and her resolve. "I believe, ma'am, I have already paid more than many would dare."

"I do agree, sweet woman. You are a treasure any man would be proud to claim as his own. Do you want him?"

Liesel did not know whether to laugh or shout. "Ma'am, are you asking me if I would marry your son?"

"Of course I am. I have only one son. One child whose happiness I am devoted to. One heir whose welfare I wish to secure. One man who has done more for this country and for those in other countries than many in the royal family." She tipped her head. "So I ask you, can you live with him and love him as he deserves, if he can wipe away the false accusations that have kept him from me and from his home?"

"I would like nothing more than to live in peace and quiet in the shade of tall oak trees and never go farther than my garden gate."

"No royal courts?"

Liesel shook her head once.

"No royal marriage?" Lady Fournier gave her a sidelong glance.

Liesel smiled. "No."

"No return to Vaillancourt's kitchen?"

Ah. Dirk's mother had learned much from him. "I really do not like peeling garlic, my lady."

Lady Fournier's smile was there and gone in the blink of an eye. "Hmmm. And have you thought at all about the enormous amount of cajoling you must do in order to persuade the Queen of Great Britain to tear up your engagement agreement to the Duke of Isenhurst?"

Liesel fought the terror that Lady Fournier's questions wrought, but she thrilled to the fact that they had been asked. "I have contemplated that, ma'am. I have nothing more than my evidence that I did work for Clive, the Marquess of Carlisle, in Paris and peeled garlic for Bonaparte's deputy minister of the interior."

"And your attempt to save the Duke of Enghien."

"And that."

"And that you were assaulted by the Duke of Isenhurst when no more than a girl."

"True."

"And that Isenhurst attempted to kidnap you to take you to the altar."

"Yes, that also."

"The queen must know, my dear. No one treats a lady, royal

or not, like baggage to be deposited on the altar of her denigration!"

"I will go to her, my lady. I have planned it. First, I had to see Clive—Lord Carlisle. I did that this morning. Then," she said, picking up the faded green sarcenet of her old gown, "my next step was to go beg favors from my modiste."

"A gown worthy of the queen will take days to sew."

"Oh, she is good. Such a dress might take her just two days."

"I have taken the liberty of engaging my own dressmaker for you." Lady Fournier lifted the tiny watch pinned as a brooch to her bodice. "At four. Here."

Liesel grinned at her new friend. "That is kind of you, my lady."

"Necessary, dearest. We must call upon the queen tomorrow."

"We?" Liesel had to be sure she'd heard correctly.

"Of course, Liesel. I may call you Liesel, may I not?"

"Oh yes." Her hopes flew about her drawing room like butterflies fresh from their cocoon. She pressed her hands together. "The queen thinks of me as a crazed bluestocking with aspirations of spinsterhood."

"The educated woman you are now has a reason to marry, does she not?"

"Only one man, my lady."

"And a very fine one at that. So I ask you, shall you and I go the queen, Liesel?"

"For you to join me to call upon Her Majesty would be beyond my dreams."

"Well, my dear Liesel, you have accomplished for me what I never thought possible. You have inspired my darling son to find a way to come to his home and live out his days here, where he belongs."

"I have done so little, my lady."

"My name, my dear, is Charlotte. Please use it. What you have done is an enormously vital thing, Liesel. You love my son.

And for his love you will reject influence abroad to work here beside him. That is no small thing. To love a man who was reviled, threatened, an outcast, and to love him so well that he is compelled to find ways to change all of that, you have done a wondrous thing. You have made all our days to come a heaven on earth."

This, from a woman whose acquaintance with Liesel could be measured only in minutes, washed away all but one trepidation about the future here in her adopted country.

"Well, then, Charlotte," she managed as she fought her second set of tears today, "I think I must summon my butler to bring us something to celebrate our new friendship."

"My dear girl, I do like the way you think. Might we have him fetch us a good bottle of whisky?"

Chapter Nineteen

Fournier Park
Kent, England
June 30, 1804

LIESEL HAD RETURNED south to Fournier Park with the baroness after meeting with Queen Charlotte. She'd occupied herself each day enjoying the company of her hostess, her brother, and her sister. When she needed a mindful pursuit, she visited the library for a book. The collection was vast. She felt like a child in a sweet shop. When she needed exercise, she went down to the tenants' cottages, where she made a new friend each day, and helped weeding and planting their kitchen gardens.

But when she needed something to take her mind from the question of where in the world Dirk Fournier might be, she went down to the park's kitchens. She did not tell the baroness. Such a thing was not done by a lady, much less a princess.

Still Liesel needed the release. She fretted over Dirk's actions. But if that were not enough, she ground her teeth over Carlisle's disturbing news that Mara and Hartenburg had been greeted by his father not with congratulations, but with condemnation. Liesel prayed Mara had the tools to deal with such rudeness.

"No wonder I need something lively," she muttered to herself as she took the back stairs down to the kitchen. There, Cook and her two maids were at first shocked to see her don an apron.

They were further stunned to see her wield knives over vegetables and meat like a convicted cutthroat. She returned the compliment of the surprise when she taught the three of them how to make an apple *tarte tatin*. When they tasted her wares, licked their lips…and did not die, they welcomed her offer to teach them how to make a French stew. They were shocked when they loved it.

"Must be the red wine," said the first kitchen maid.

"Must be the beef," said the second.

"Must be the garlic," said Cook with a wink.

What drove Liesel's impatience were newspaper articles she read each day full of the whereabouts of Dirk. He had arrived from Bremen, via Yarmouth, and gone down to his home in Kent. Almost immediately thereafter, he had journeyed to London, dining with Miss Scarlett Hawthorne in a large party at her home, and later alone with the prime minister.

Word was that he'd then journeyed north. Some said he visited his childhood friend Tate, Lord Appleby, and that man's new wife in Norfolk. Others said they spotted a man who resembled Lord Fournier in Manchester.

Why he should be there caused great speculation, declared one rag, *but we, Dear Reader, have no confirmation of this.*

A different story brought a smile to Liesel's lips. A public declaration to a newspaper in Manchester was issued by Lord Fellowes and his new wife, Alice. The public apology to Lord Fournier became a most repeated story in newspapers from London to Dublin, and even so far as Boston, Massachusetts.

A smaller story also appeared. A holding company, recently begun, had failed to attract enough capital to fulfill the orders of three new ships. The company proposed to begin the triangular trade along the Atlantic. Many questioned the wisdom of adding more trade, which so many recognized was inhuman, to that route.

Liesel read of her own actions in similar papers.

As for news of Crown Princess Elizabeth of Rittenburg, she was the guest of Lady Fournier in London recently. While there, the two of them called upon the queen.

In gossip sheets, it was rumored that *…the princess, lately traveling in her native land, had done service to the Crown during her time abroad. She currently resides in the country, awaiting the renovation of a new house she has purchased for the benefit of her brother, sister, and herself. Both siblings will now reside with the princess here in England.*

Only Charlotte, Lady Fournier, and the servants at Fournier Park knew that Liesel and her family lived there. Liesel's new wardrobe, bits of which arrived daily from Charlotte's modiste, made her set for company she was yet to enjoy. The elaborate new gown of pink satin and white lace, which she wore to the Queen's House that day she and Charlotte visited, was put away. She had the distinct impression she would not be invited back to Buckingham anytime soon.

But now she spent her days wondering when Dirk might appear. Aside from the note he'd given to his mother to deliver to her, Liesel had heard nothing from him. Even that note was far too brief.

Dearest Liesel,

Wait for me. —Dirk

Had she not been doing that for months?

The man irritated her. How long did he need? She, on the other hand, required no days or nights to make his restitution more acceptable to her. He had always been the noblest creature she'd ever had the honor to know.

Meanwhile, he stayed away while the *ton* took their sweet time ruminating? Good God, did he not realize that they would tittle-tattle to each other for *years*?

She groused about his delay in the privacy of her rooms. She walked the floor. She walked his land. She laughed with his tenants. She peeled garlic in his kitchen. Each day, she vowed that when he did arrive home, for making her wait so long, she would box his ears!

She missed him.

DIRK HAD INSISTED that his coachman and footman *had* to make Fournier Park today. Not usually so demanding of his staff, he had now done all he could to prepare a future that suited him there. He had alerted his London house in Grosvenor Square to his impending marriage and the arrival of a new mistress. He expected that he and his bride would not venture into London, nor Society, until late in autumn. His desire to keep Liesel to himself, plus his understanding that she would not relish yet another long trip in a carriage, meant he expected that November might be the right time to appear among the *ton*.

He had no fears about that. What Scarlett and Carlton had done for him with the government and the Crown had more than polished his name. What Dáire O'Neill had done with Fellowes and Alice had more than washed the stains from his reputations. What he had done with them eased his conscience. He was not a man bent on revenge any longer.

Now he had only one goal in mind: to get to his prospective bride and marry her in front of as many people as possible. As his coach rounded the bend to the front portico of Fournier Park in the dark, the silhouette of the house beckoned him.

Handing his gloves, coat, and hat to Jameson, he glanced up the stairs and listened for the sounds of the house. "Where is everyone?"

It was past ten o'clock, so he expected the children to be asleep, his mother to be in her rooms—and Liesel to be in bed.

That was exactly where his vivid imagination had taken him in the hours since he'd left London.

Jameson responded with all those locations Dirk had predicted for everyone.

"Wonderful," he said, and took the grand staircase two steps at a time.

"But my lord…?"

Dirk paused at the landing. "Yes?"

"Do you wish dinner, brandy, or a bath?"

"I will ring when I've decided, Jameson." He took the steps up to the second floor and headed for Liesel's rooms.

He had so much to tell her, so much joy to reveal, that he was bursting with news. So when he knocked and no one answered, he debated whether to continue. Wake her up, he could. But he doubted she'd be angry with him. She hardly ever was. His darling was so even tempered. He smiled and opened the door.

Her sitting room was dark, save for two wall sconces casting flickering lights here and there. But the sounds of what occurred in the room beyond had his mind whirling with laughter.

Of course—it was right that he should walk in on her bath!

He walked past her bedroom, headed straight for the sounds of splashing water.

The lovely coincidence was complemented by the fact that she was alone. In her bath.

"Good evening, sweetheart." He strode in her boudoir to stand before the edge of the porcelain tub, then crossed his arms, lest he rush her past her surprise—and spoil his own fun.

She gaped at him.

"You look well," he said, and could not change his rogue's tone. What he could do, however, was look.

And what he saw was everything he had desired of her. Everything he had fought to claim. Everything he'd never thought he even merited.

She noted the path of his gaze, her lips still parted in surprise. Her long arms to the rim of the tub, her elegant fingers curled around the edge, she let him look.

Oh, yes. She let him have his fill. Her golden hair billowed around her like a crown with the humidity. Long waves curved around her cheeks and down her shoulders. The arcs and planes of her slender body made his mouth water. Her unmoving acceptance of his perusal made his knees weak.

This was his Liesel. His woman filled with courage and conviction. His darling who had loved him in spite of what the world claimed he was. His madwoman who had declared her love for him when he could not declare his own for her.

"Pardon me," she said, raising her chin in royal hauteur. "Who are you, sir, to invade my boudoir so boldly?"

Looking at the ceiling, he chuckled. Then he strode toward her, all the better to hunger for her lithe figure, full breasts, slim hips, and the pale thatch of hair at the juncture of her thighs.

"I am the man who loves you."

She sank lower. Her head upon the rim of the tub, she stretched out. Her breasts bobbed in the water. Her pink nipples, growing firm, rose above the waterline. One knee bent, she tipped her head to one side as she opened her legs to him. "I'm delighted to see him."

"As I am you."

Her expression gutted him. She had missed him terribly. "Where in *hell* have you been, sir?"

Positioned as he was at the very edge of her bathtub, he spread his hands wide in supplication. "Everywhere to make it possible for you to wed me—and never be ashamed to call yourself my wife."

"Never would I have been ashamed, sir. But do tell me how you have accomplished this."

Satisfaction warmed him through and through. He unbuttoned his frock coat and threw it to the nearby chair. "I went to Scarlett Hawthorne and her chief clerk, both of whom went to the government and won me favor for the work I've done."

She slowly smiled. "Praise long overdue. What else?"

He removed his waistcoat, and it sailed over to join his coat. "I went to see a man who makes his living arranging retribution for those who have harmed others."

"A man I would like to meet."

"Someday, I will introduce you. You will like him." Dirk sat on her stool and pulled off his boots and socks. "I asked him to give me the address of Alice Sedgwick and Lord Fellowes."

"You saw them?" Apprehension drained her lovely face of any joy. "And what happened?"

He frowned, recalling the squalid conditions of their existence. "They have lost their child. She has lost her family's support. He has lost the income from his first wife. They married in Manchester a few weeks ago. While they are at last together, they are much diminished in circumstances."

"Yet they issued a public apology for their accusations."

"They did."

"Why?" Her brow wrinkled.

"Seeing me, evidently, was all they needed to call forth remorse for what they had done."

"Unusual for two so ruthless."

"It is." He would explain later, when they had more time, how he had gone to see Dáire O'Neill upon his return to London from Manchester. He'd told the man not to punish Fellowes financially. Dirk would even pay O'Neill the portion of the fee that man would have earned from Fellowes's ruin. "The two of them seem happy together. So with the loss of their child and their precarious finances, I could not make their lives worse. They were happy to post their statements in the Manchester papers."

"Many have reprinted them," Liesel said, and sat forward with a whoosh of water.

His ambition to have her wet and willing drove out all other desires. He stood, undid his flies, and pushed down his breeches and his small clothes. His desire for her was a bold, hard statement.

Her lips spread wide in a grin as he took a step to stand near her.

Her hand cupped his hip.

His manhood showed how he appreciated the caress.

She licked her lips.

"I'm coming in." He lifted a leg over and put his foot in the tub between her thighs.

"Oh," she said, her gaze on the long, hard sight before her. "Do you think you'll fit?"

He put another foot in. "I know I will."

She giggled, but when faced with the insistent evidence of his desire for her, she paused and whispered, "I remember."

He bent down and lifted her to her feet. He wrapped his arms around her, one hand to her derrière, and pressed. "So do I. This time, what we do will be complete."

She blinked, her amethyst eyes locking on his. "Do you promise?"

"From now on, everything we do together will be the fulfillment of how I love you and you love me."

Tears sprang to her lower lids. "Clive has relieved me of work abroad. The queen has released me from Isenhurst."

"I know. I read." He grinned and rubbed the tip of his nose on hers. "Mama sent letters to our Grosvenor Square house every day." He wended one hand down her throat to one breast, her hip, then threaded his fingers into the soft hair between her thighs. "I read them all as I arrived last week."

She drew in air as he parted her folds and sought the core of her. Wet and hot, she was all that he needed, and he'd give her all she required.

"Dirk." She said his name like a prayer and nuzzled into his shoulder. "Why, my darling, were you so damn long in London?"

He stepped out of the tub, her hand in his, picked up a towel on a bench and flung it over her, then walked backward, leading her toward her bedroom.

At the edge of the bed, he urged her down and knelt before her. One day he had promised her, in her family's throne room, that he was her liege man, and he wished to prove it once and for all. "I went to my bankers."

At the mention of such a mundane thing, she blinked. "I don't understand."

"I am more than solvent."

She said, "Excellent," though she appeared uncertain what more that implied.

"I told him I intend to remain at home and that I resume all my obligations to my family and my estate."

"As you should."

"As I wish to do for the rest of my life."

She waited, speculation in her beautiful eyes.

He pulled the towel more firmly around her and rubbed her arms dry. "Then, the other day, I called upon the archbishop."

This took her frown away. "Of Canterbury?"

"I told him of a lady who'd saved me from the wilderness, who loved me when few others did."

She gulped. "Did he ask who this woman was?"

"Oh yes. I told him she was my darling, my princess, and if he would consent, I wanted her to become my wife and my baroness."

"What did he say?"

"That I am a very fortunate man."

She put her arms around his shoulders and her legs around his hips.

He grinned and nestled closer to her warm invitation. "I have from him a special license to marry you."

Tears dribbled down her cheeks.

"Oh, sweetheart," he whispered, kissing her tears away. "Will you marry me?"

"How can you doubt it?" She sniffed as she hugged him closer.

He kissed her ear, her throat, and then took her lips in a fierce claim. "Tomorrow?"

"No!"

"But—"

She gave an exasperated cry. "If you think I will let you go tonight, you are so wrong."

He chuckled. "A demanding wife."

"Exactly. And I do not wish to go to my wedding having guests say I looked like a…a…bag!"

He snorted. "Hag?"

"That, yes."

He laughed and nuzzled the hollow behind her ear. Then he froze and pulled back to look down at her. "But you *will* marry me?"

"I will." She cupped his firm jaw. "I have never wanted any other man."

"I have never wanted any other woman. You, my darling, are my love, my everything. Only you."

Chapter Twenty

Their wedding three days hence was to occur in the parlor with the guests who'd accepted the hand-written invitations of Charlotte, Lady Fournier. Dozens replied in the affirmative to coming down from London. Fournier Park was to bulge with guests, their servants, their carriages, and horses too.

"All but the queen will attend," said Charlotte, Liesel's soon-to-be mother-in-law, at dinner one night before the guests were to descend.

"I don't mind. I hope you don't."

"No, my dear." The lady lifted her wine glass in a toast. "I am pleased she refrained. As reward for my years of being at her beck and call, I am pleased."

Liesel sat quite still. "She gave us what we need when we called on her. In fact, I will be content if I am never called to court again."

"You may yet be, my dear," Charlotte said as she smiled at her, then her son. "The queen forgives. She understands love." Then the baroness picked up her fork and knife and paused. "By the way, Cook told me a tale today that I was shocked to hear." She took a bite of her *pot-au-feu* and munched with delight.

"What was that, Mama?" Dirk asked.

"I understand that we have a new kitchen hand who graces us

with her services occasionally," she replied with raised brows.

"We do." Liesel put her utensils down and waited for the reprimand to never set foot in the kitchen again.

"She does a marvelous *pot-au-feu*." Charlotte's dark eyes flared with humor. "Quite a bit of garlic, don't you think?"

Liesel was mortified. "Oh, ma'am, that new maid can leave out all the garlic next time."

"Really? Hmmm." The baroness mulled that over, took another bite, swallowed it, and looked confused. "I rather think the pot needs more. Don't you, Dirk?"

"I do indeed, Mama." He chuckled.

"I enjoyed her brioche the other day. No garlic, of course. But I do wonder if this maid comes around often. Have you any idea, Liesel?"

Liesel hesitated. Should she tell Charlotte now that she *was* the maid?

Dirk piped up. "I think, Mama, she will soon become a permanent member of the household."

"Thank God for that," said the baroness, tucking back into her stew. Then she added, "I wonder. Does she do *sauerbraten*?"

⇉⇉⟩✦⟨⇇⇇

ANOTHER TWO MORNINGS later, Liesel entered the parlor exactly at ten o'clock. It was crowded in every inch with those she knew and many she did not. Nikky and Katrin walked on either side of her. Katrin was her maid of honor. Nikky stood for Rainer and was to give her hand to Dirk.

At her appearance, the guests murmured their approval and parted as Dirk strode forward, his hand out to Nikky. Her brother gave her over with a grin. She let Dirk lead her to the vicar. He had not come to her last night, saying it was not appropriate for them to be together. But she had tried to sleep without him and failed. By the wee hours, she had made her way to his bedroom and crawled in beside him. As always, he had awakened and taken her in his arms. Then, as he had the previous two nights, he'd led her into memorable hours of ecstasy.

Now, as he faced her with a grin, his eyes danced with the same desire he'd shown her time and again. "Never will you want for safety, peace, and this man who loves you."

"I will love you beyond my last breath."

"So then," he whispered as he lifted her hands to his lips, "marry me, my darling. Our future awaits."

She took those words as their vows, but happily recited the words the vicar gave them anyway.

THROUGHOUT THE BREAKFAST reception, Dirk traced his wife's steps as she greeted and conversed with their guests. His wife was a vision of serenity as she laughed with everyone. Scarlett Hawthorne and her man, Todd Carlton, had come together, though even his mother knew to give instructions to Jameson that they sleep in separate rooms. Lord and Lady Ashley plus Lord and Lady Ramsey had come, too. Lord Appleby had declined for himself and his wife. She was expecting their first child in a few weeks and dared not leave home to ride in a carriage for days. But they sent their congratulations and an invitation to join them in London next spring.

Dirk, grateful his friends had descended upon the park in such numbers, was thrilled to see Liesel's friends come as well. A young widow who had attended the girls' finishing school with Liesel had arrived yesterday.

Lord Carlisle, Liesel's contact in the Foreign Office, had appeared late last night. A devil-may-care-looking creature, Carlisle—Dirk recalled—had made a name for himself as an expert in protection of the southern coast. His father had been a naval captain and had engendered love of the sea in his son.

Though Carlisle had never gone to the navy, he nonetheless was an expert fisherman and sailor. What was more, all that sunshine had honed his body into a muscular machine and turned his brown hair into shocks streaked with gold and platinum.

Dirk noted how Carlisle greeted his new wife with a kiss to her hand. His possessiveness stirred. Never having encountered her in the presence of another eligible man, Dirk marveled in that most elemental way that she had chosen him.

He strode over to them, impatient to take her away from them all.

Minutes later, he led her up the stairs into their new suite and pressed her to the closed door. "I wanted to kiss my wife."

She caressed his cheeks and grinned. "How good of you. You waited so long to take me away, I worried that my husband may have wearied of me already."

He traced her lower lip with his thumb. "That will never happen."

AND SO BARON Fournier kept his new wife well occupied the rest of that day and night. Their guests did not inquire as to their whereabouts, wishing to be discreet. The next morning, he and she left for Brighton. It was a short trip, and his bride was most grateful for its brevity, even when the coachman pulled up to their hotel and interrupted Dirk's scintillating seduction of his new wife.

The wedding of Baron Fournier to the Crown Princess of Rittenburg was a topic of many articles in international newspapers for many weeks afterward.

All described how Lord Fournier had recently been cleared of all wrongdoing by the two who had tried to blackmail and defame him. Most went on to report that the baron was devoted to the German princess who was now his baroness. That their marriage had been blessed by the Crown. Few mentioned the princess once had been betrothed to a member of the royal family.

However, the baron gave not a fiddle for any of the news. He was free, his life was orderly, and his beloved was his.

He and his wife returned to London in early November. The dowager Baroness Fournier did not go to Town. She remained at the park because she was preparing to move to the dower house near the southern coast. The newly married couple, as was the custom, called upon their friends and others in Society. Their visits were brief, as it was whispered that the new Baroness Fournier appeared to be a few months with child.

Nonetheless, in many Society columns, the couple let it be known they were both at home to anyone who wished to call.

Their journeys abroad were finished. They were tending home fires only.

The challenge continues...

About the Author

Cerise DeLand loves to write about dashing heroes and the sassy women they adore. Whether she's penning historical romances or contemporaries, she has received praise for her poetic elegance and accuracy of detail.

An award-winning author of more than 50 novels, she's been published since 1991 by Pocket Books, St. Martin's Press, Kensington and independent presses. Her books have been monthly selections of the Doubleday Book Club and the Mystery Guild. Plus she's won nominations and awards for Best Historical of the Year, Best Regency and scores of rave reviews from *Romantic Times, Affair de Coeur, Publisher's Weekly* and more.

To research, she's dived into the oldest texts and dustiest library shelves. She's also traveled abroad, trusty notebook and pen in hand, to visit the chateaux and country homes she loves to people with her own imaginary characters.

And at home every day? She loves to cook, hates to dust, goes swimming at least once a week and tries (desperately) to grow vegetables in her arid backyard in south Texas!

www.ingramcontent.com/pod-product-compliance
Lightning Source LLC
Chambersburg PA
CBHW060403310726
48976CB00003B/932